Emma Lajeunesse Albani, 1847-1930.

Artist: Francine Auger

Michelle Labrèche-Larouche

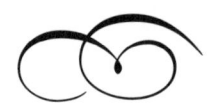

Michelle Labrèche-Larouche has always loved music and writing. She studied the piano throughout her childhood, and published her first article in *Châtelaine* magazine in 1964. For over twenty years, she has worked full-time for *Châtelaine* as researcher, journalist, and editor of different sections. She is now responsible for the Arts and Entertainment section. During the 1970s, she was also editor-in-chief of the cultural events monthly, *Montréal ce mois-ci*. She has interviewed artists and performers on many occasions. She has a deep knowledge of the Quebec theatrical milieu and has maintained an abiding interest in the classical music scene.

The translator: Darcy Dunton

Darcy Dunton left Ottawa for Montreal after graduating from high school and, three decades later, still enjoys her adoptive city for the exceptional cultural opportunities that it offers. She obtained a Licence ès Lettres and a M.Sc. in anthropology from the Université de Montréal, and has worked as a translator since 1978.

THE QUEST LIBRARY
is edited by
Rhonda Bailey

The Editorial Board is composed of
Lynne Bowen
Janet Lunn
T.F. Rigelhof

Editorial correspondence:
Rhonda Bailey, Editorial Director
XYZ Publishing
P.O. Box 250
Lantzville BC
V0R 2H0
E-mail: xyzed@shaw.ca

In the same collection

Ven Begamudré, *Isaac Brock: Larger Than Life*.
Lynne Bowen, *Robert Dunsmuir: Laird of the Mines*.
Kate Braid, *Emily Carr: Rebel Artist*.
William Chalmers, *George Mercer Dawson: Geologist, Scientist, Explorer*.
Judith Fitzgerald, *Marshall McLuhan: Wise Guy*.
Stephen Eaton Hume, *Frederick Banting: Hero, Healer, Artist*.
Naïm Kattan, *A.M. Klein: Poet and Prophet*.
Betty Keller, *Pauline Johnson: First Aboriginal Voice of Canada*.
Dave Margoshes, *Tommy Douglas: Building the New Society*.
Raymond Plante, *Jacques Plante: Behind the Mask*.
T.F. Rigelhof, *George Grant: Redefining Canada*.
Arthur Slade, *John Diefenbaker. An Appointment with Destiny*.
John Wilson, *John Franklin: Traveller on Undiscovered Seas*.
John Wilson, *Norman Bethune: A Life of Passionate Conviction*.
Rachel Wyatt, *Agnes Macphail: Champion of the Underdog*.

Emma Albani

Copyright © 1994 Michelle Labrèche-Larouche and XYZ éditeur.
English translation copyright © Darcy Dunton and XYZ Publishing

All rights reserved. The use of any part of this publication reproduced, transmitted in any form or by any means, electronic, mechanical, photocopying, recording, or otherwise, or stored in a retrieval system without the prior written consent of the publisher – or, in the case of photocopying or other reprographic copying, a licence from Canadian Copyright Licensing Agency – is an infringement of the copyright law.

Canadian Cataloguing in Publication Data
Labrèche-Larouche, Michelle, 1938-
    Emma Albani: international star
    (The Quest Library ; 16).
    Translation of Emma Albani: la diva, la vedette mondiale.
    Includes bibliographical references and index.
    ISBN 0-9688166-9-X

    1. Albani, Emma, Dame. 2. Singers – Quebec (Province) – Biography.
I. Dunton, Darcy. II. Title. III. Series: Quest library; 16.

ML420.A5L32 2001   782.4218092   C2001-941201-0

Legal Deposit: Fourth quarter 2001
National Library of Canada
Bibliothèque nationale du Québec

XYZ Publishing acknowledges the support of The Quest Library project by the Canadian Studies Program and the Book Publishing Industry Development Program (BPIDP) of the Department of Canadian Heritage. The opinions expressed do not necessarily reflect the views of the Government of Canada.

The publishers further acknowledge the financial support our publishing program receives from The Canada Council for the Arts, the ministère de la Culture et des Communications du Québec, and the Société de développement des entreprises culturelles.

Chronology and photo research: Michèle Vanasse
Index: Darcy Dunton
Layout: Édiscript enr.
Cover design: Zirval Design
Cover illustration: Francine Auger

Printed and bound in Canada

XYZ Publishing   Distributed by:
1781 Saint Hubert Street   General Distribution Services
Montreal, Quebec H2L 3Z1   325 Humber College Boulevard
Tel: (514) 525-2170   Toronto, Ontario M9W 7C3
Fax: (514) 525-7537   Tel: (416) 213-1919
E-mail: xyzed@mlink.net   Fax: (416) 213-1917
Web site: www.xyzedit.com   E-mail: cservice@genpub.com

MICHELLE LABRÈCHE-LAROUCHE

ALBANI

Emma

INTERNATIONAL STAR

XYZ Publishing

Acknowledgments

The author would like to thank Annette Rémondière for her precious assistance with the research for this book, as well as Jean Daigle, Claude Fournier, and Edgar Fruitier for their helpful suggestions and advice. Finally, my warmest thanks to my family and friends for their support during the writing of the book.

*To my son, Marc,
and his father, Gaëtan Labrèche,
another great artist.*

Contents

Introduction	1
1 A Regal Gift	3
2 "You'll be a musician, my child."	19
3 One Day, My Prince Will Come	31
4 In the Land of Bel Canto	47
5 Happy Days in Europe	59
6 A Disturbing Character: the Tsar	73
7 Travelling the Paths of Glory	87
8 Happiness in London, Fiasco in Milan	101
9 The Star Pales	117
10 The Curtain Falls	131
Epilogue	145
Chronology of Emma Albani (1847-1930)	147
Bibliography/Discography	173
Index	175

Introduction

Before the arrival of Céline Dion, there were other international singing stars from Quebec. The first of these was Emma Lajeunesse, alias Emma Albani, who, like Céline, started her career when she was very young. Albani was one of the greatest opera sopranos of the Victorian era; the 150th anniversary of her birth coincided with the year of publication of this book (1994 in the original French-language version). I have approached the long life and career of this fascinating character by recreating episodes that I felt were significant, using impressionistic touches.

The great divas have always been goddesses in the eyes of their fans, especially in the days when few recordings existed, and those that were available were of poor quality.

I hope you like my heroine as much as I did.

M.L.-L.

Victoria, Queen of Great Britain and Ireland, and Empress of India, was Emma Albani's great friend and protector.

1

A Regal Gift

"Albert, my dearest, my beloved husband for all eternity, is it truly you?" asked the diminutive figure enveloped in a full-length black dress, in a low, tremulous voice, her eyes raised heavenward. The white lace cap holding back her silver hair gave her a half-dramatic, half-comic air. The atmosphere in the room was charged with feeling.

Moonbeams penetrated between the heavy crimson velvet curtains looped in gold braid, and the flames in the huge fireplace sent menacing shadows flickering and leaping on the walls. The ceiling was so high that it could almost be confused with the night sky. The few tapers burning atop the silver candelabrum added to the aura of mystical expectancy. In a corner of this vast room, in which an unsuccessful attempt had been made at creating warmth and intimacy, reigned a grand piano draped in a cashmere coverlet. All the pieces of furniture – chesterfields, armchairs, and cabinets – were massive and seemed to have been in the same position for centuries. Bookshelves crammed with hundreds of volumes separated panelled walls hung with drawings by the great masters and a Holbein portrait of Queen Bess. Low mahogany stepladders were placed about the room to allow access to the books on the highest shelves.

The little old lady in black sitting at the low, round table was Victoria Regina, Queen of England, Scotland, and Ireland. Her knobby hands were placed on the tabletop, fingers spread apart and palms pressed downwards. On her right, she touched fingers with her lady-in-waiting, the dowager Lady Erroll. Both women were gloved. Lady Erroll, immobile and distinguished in her silvery mauve gown and ropes of pearls, was as pale as her hair; in this beyond-the-grave setting, she might have been a ghost.

The little finger of the Queen's left hand touched the finger of another, much younger woman whose angelic face was set off by a crown of dark curls. Her eyes were grey-blue; she was slim, of medium height, and was dressed in white. She seemed to be surrounded by a halo of ethereal light.

She was Albani,[1] one of the great opera divas of the age. In that year, 1876, she was at the height of her

---

1. Opera fans often refer to their idols by their last names, for example, Melba, Patti, Albani, Caruso, Callas, Stratas, Pavarotti.

International Star

glory, singing the full season at London's Covent Garden Theatre, officially called The Royal Italian Opera. After several European and American tours, she had achieved world fame and success – and royal favour.

Albani's presence among the heaven-born was nonetheless surprising. She was of humble origin, born Rose-Marie-Emma Lajeunesse in Chambly, a small town surrounded by farms in Lower Canada, on November 1, 1847 – twenty-eight years ago. Officially, however, she was only twenty-four: female *artistes* usually subtracted a few years from their ages, without anyone raising an eyebrow.

From an early age, Emma had clearly been destined for an illustrious career. But she had never imagined that one day she would find herself in Windsor Castle, sitting with Victoria, Queen of Great Britain and Empress of India! Nor could she ever have conceived of participating in a séance with Her Majesty, who was trying to establish contact with her husband and cousin, Albert of Saxe-Coburg, who had died fifteen years before.

"What a strange situation," Emma thought. She had not yet grown accustomed to the fact that the Queen frequently requested her presence and had honoured her with her friendship; it made her feel radiant and proud. Albani was, in fact, the only vocalist on whom the sovereign had bestowed such a marked partiality. The singer's breast swelled with emotion under her lace bodice.

At the same time, the young woman was uneasy: what was going to happen in this communication with the other world? Would the visiting spirit about to manifest itself reveal something terrifying to her, Emma? What if she learned that she would lose her beautiful voice?

Only one gentleman was included in the select party: it was Sir Thomas Biddulph, one of dead Prince Albert's squires, smooth-bearded and dressed in a severe black frock coat. "Answer, spirit, I enjoin you," he whispered urgently. "If your answer is no, knock once. If it is yes, knock twice." The members of the small assembly waited in silence, their pallid faces frozen in expectancy and their bodies tense. They might have been mortuary statues in an underground vault. The seconds stretched into minutes that felt unbearably long. The beating of the participants' hearts was almost audible.

Suddenly, the table seemed to elevate and one of its legs sounded twice on the parquet floor. "You know the alphabetical code," continued Sir Thomas excitedly, addressing the summoned spirit. "You would not deprive Her Majesty your wife of the comfort she requires to continue to live without you," he urged.

The table began to "speak," emitting twelve taps for the letter *f*, nine for the letter *r*, gradually spelling out *f-r-e-e-y-o-u-r-s-e-l-f*. "Free yourself!" the company exclaimed in unison. At that moment, the tabletop tilted to touch the Queen's thighs, brushing them with the gentleness of a caress. Victoria closed her eyes and brief, gasping cries escaped her, resembling the sobbing of a little girl. Her sobs ended in a scream. Shudders ran through the other witnesses of this calling-up of the dead.

The table righted itself and became inert. The consoled widow spoke in a drained voice: "My love, we are separated forever, but from the realm of the shadows, you repeat to me, as you ever did in life, 'My dear, we can do nothing about it.' And as you thus give me your leave, I will break the vow I made for the love and respect of your memory, to never go to the theatre, to concerts, or to the opera."

Silence fell over the room with the effect of a dead weight. Then, slowly, the tension dissipated. Victoria came back to the world of the living and took up her cold mask of imperial autocracy again. The evening's séance was at an end. Lady Erroll lit a lamp and addressed her queen: "Sir Thomas is a quite extraordinary medium. I vastly prefer him to that rather sinister character who is so much in vogue, Mr. Hume – the one who officiates for the Duchess of York."

"Your Majesty," dared Thomas Biddulph, "I believe your husband would wish you to attend Madame Albani's next performance."

"I will dedicate it to you, Your Highness," said Emma, curtseying to the Queen.

Victoria declined to acknowledge the compliment. She rose to her feet and declared:

"We are tired."

"God save the Queen!" chorused the others as she left the room.

Outside, a spring breeze stirred the smaller branches of the century-old oaks on the castle grounds and rippled the surface of the nearby Thames. Across the river, the students of venerable Eton College were sleeping soundly, never suspecting that their haughty sovereign, in emulation of several high society ladies, was giving herself over to making tables move.

On July 25, 1876, Albani was welcomed onto the stage of the Royal Albert Hall. The curtain rose, and amid thundering applause, the diva stepped forward. She glanced up at the royal box. Her friend Victoria was there, surrounded by members of her family. Emma's eyes filled with tears as she was warmed by the thought, "The Queen appreciates me; I have conquered!"

On the following day, the soprano received a letter from Victoria's secretary:

> *Buckingham Palace,*
> *July 26, 1876*
> *The Queen asked me to write you to tell you how much Her Majesty was enchanted by your singing last night at the Royal Albert Hall. The Queen affirms that it was perfect and that Her Majesty was able to distinguish every note of your splendid voice. I regret very much not to have had the time to visit you, as the Queen returns to Windsor today, but I am certain that you will be happy to know how much the Queen appreciated you and that it was such a success.*
>
> *Believe me, sincerely yours,*
> *Jane Ely*

The friendship between Emma Albani and Queen Victoria was not a recent development. The two women had met two years earlier in the British capital.

International Star

∞

At the beginning of the summer of 1874, the young operatic soprano, Emma Lajeunesse, alias Emma Albani, was attracting considerable attention in England. The Queen had been intrigued to hear of this young Canadian singer, already an opera star – the first from the colonies to have achieved such a notable success in Europe – and wanted to meet her. For Emma, her first introduction to Victoria was unforgettable. Ever afterwards, she would recall it in sharp detail.

On June 24, 1876, a coach emblazoned with the royal arms stopped in front of the Cavendish Hotel in London. This was where Emma Albani was staying with her sister Cornélia, or "Nelly," and their father, Joseph Lajeunesse – who had taken to calling himself Monsieur de St. Louis to fit in with the aristocratic entourage of his celebrated daughter.

"A letter from Her Majesty, the Queen," announced the royal messenger, handing over a sealed envelope. The two sisters were struck dumb. To examine the contents of the missive, they took it into the drawing room of their suite.

This room was furnished with well-padded poufs, ornate ebony chests of drawers, gracefully gathered striped drapes, and large plant stands inlaid with oriental motifs. On the walls were several landscape paintings depicting bucolic country scenes. Here, the grand piano occupied the place of honour, taking up the centre of the room; it was graced by a photograph of Tsar Alexander II, in a frame studded with diamonds and incorporating the imperial eagle of the Romanoffs. A

Emma Albani

flattering dedication to Miss Albani was written on the photograph itself. In a second gilt frame was a portrait of Maman at the piano in the Lajeunesse home in Chambly. A group portrait showed little Emma and Cornélia with their father, and various other mounted photographs commemorated triumphs of Emma's career in the opera houses of Messina, Malta, and London. This souvenir gallery was completed by a number of original sketches of opera sets and costumes.

Emma opened the envelope and caught her breath.

"The Queen has invited me to sing for her at Windsor Castle! What will Papa say?" she asked Cornélia, while prancing in delight, her eyes aglow. "And what will I wear?"

"Your white dress," Cornélia answered promptly. "With the Valenciennes lace bodice, and Maman's cameo. Wear it around your neck on a cerise velvet ribbon. It will be your lucky charm."

"And you'll wear your dove-grey dress. You'll carry my scores and accompany me on the piano, as usual."

"As usual!" parroted Cornélia.

A long week passed.

On the afternoon of July 1, the clock in the entrance hall of the hotel suite chimed three o'clock. The two sisters took the lift downstairs; the swaying little elevator frightened them but they felt that they should get used to this new invention. Their hearts were beating fast: they were on their way to meet the Queen of England! Outside the hotel, they hailed a cab.

"To Windsor Castle!" Emma ordered proudly.

"Yes'm," was the plump cabby's unruffled response.

The city was resplendent on that sunny summer afternoon. The parks were at their greenest, and roses bloomed riotously against the brick walls of the town houses in the better sections of London. Imposing pillared façades paraded by like a row of postcards. Elegant ladies strolled languidly along the sidewalks, their magnolia complexions protected from the sun by light-coloured parasols. Hawkers, vendors, and other working people ran across the paths of moving vehicles and crowded onto tramways covered with advertisements.

"Thank goodness it's not raining!" remarked Cornélia, adding, "Summers at home are so much nicer!"

"That's true, Nelly, but there's no opera house worthy of the name at home," replied her sister. "I can't imagine going back to live there."

"But it's our country, Emma. You seem to forget that we're French Canadian!"

They were nearing their destination. Emma had butterflies in her stomach. At the palace gates, a soldier on guard stopped them. "Her Majesty is expecting us," said Emma, holding out her invitation. The wrought-iron barrier slid up and the carriage proceeded. At the entrance of the castle, a bevy of servants received the sisters and escorted them along interminable corridors.

In the royal library they were met by a lady-in-waiting to the Queen. Victoria soon appeared and was greeted by a double curtsey.

"We welcome you," she said. "This is Dame Lady Erroll, my lady-in-waiting."

"We are very much honoured, Your Majesty," answered Emma. "Allow me to introduce my sister, Cornélia Lajeunesse, who is also my accompanist."

"We are pleased to receive such a beautiful *artiste*," said the Queen with a charming smile.

Another lady was announced; her appearance provoked a spontaneous exclamation of delight from the Lajeunesse sisters.

"Mrs. Rich – you! – here!" cried Emma.

"Her Majesty did me the honour of inviting me, as I am Lady Erroll's sister, and because we three were acquainted in Malta," explained Mrs. Rich.

The happy effusions over, tea arrived and everyone was seated. The silver tea service sparkled. Sandwiches and the traditional scones lay on a laddered tray of flowered porcelain.

The conversation quickly became a friendly dialogue between the Queen and the young singer, with Lady Erroll, Mrs. Rich, and Cornélia looking on.

"How did you find Russia, my child?" asked the sovereign.

"What a magnificent country, Your Majesty! It was a great honour for me to be invited to sing at the Imperial Opera and at your son's wedding last winter. His Royal Highness the Duke of Edinburgh and Her Imperial Highness Grand Duchess Marie Alexandrovna, the Tsar's daughter, made a splendid couple! It was a wonderful evening, like something in a picture book."

"From where I was sitting at the Imperial table, I couldn't hear your voice as well as I would have liked.

International Star

Nevertheless, I appreciated your beauty, your bearing, and your interpretation of the music. It was the first time I saw you."

"The other singers were distracted by the noise – all those fanfares and trumpet blasts before every toast, the talking, the clinking of glasses, cutlery, and plates. When I sing, none of this can disturb me."

Victoria smiled, encouraging the young woman to continue in her rush of enthusiasm.

"I will never forget the magnificence of the great White Room of the Winter Palace in St. Petersburg: its hugeness, all the gold, the hundreds of lamps and candles, the beautiful marquetry floors."

"Rather ostentatious, I quite agree," remarked Victoria with a hint of irony in her voice.

Emma gabbled on.

"All the ladies in their embroidered velvet robes, their heads crowned by tiaras, their necks and arms glittering with jewels. And the dresses with gold and silver trains, fringed with lace. Then, when the evening was over, the guests covered in sable capes, hailing their coachmen who had been waiting all night. If it weren't for those huge furnaces burning in the square, they would surely have frozen to death! As for me, the Tsar was very generous," she added, lowering her eyes and blushing.

"Everything is so excessive in Russia," pronounced the monarch, who appeared not to have noticed her guest's last remark. "The cold, the wealth and the poverty, and the exaggerated enthusiasms."

"I was speaking out of turn, I fear, Your Majesty. Please forgive me."

"Not at all, my dear. Your capacity for wonder enchants us. And you, Cornélia, were you also on the trip?"

"Yes, Your Majesty, but I did not go out very often... except when Emma needed me, of course," Cornélia replied demurely.

"You studied opera in Milan and Paris, Mademoiselle Albani," said the Queen, tactfully changing the subject. "Paris... my husband and I were there in 1855 to visit the Exhibition as guests of Napoléon III. What a charming man! The Empress Eugénie prepared an apartment for us; it was so well appointed that we felt as if we were at home at Windsor! 'The only thing missing is our little dog,' we said. And three days later, we were greeted by his joyful barking! The Emperor had him brought over post-haste from England!

"And what receptions! At a ball at the Hôtel de Ville, an Arab prince knelt before us, lifted our skirt and kissed us on the calf, crying *'Honni soit qui mal y pense!'*[1] We were quite petrified at first, but after a moment, we had to bite our lips to prevent ourselves from bursting out laughing."

The others smiled.

"But you have come here to sing for us, Mademoiselle Albani," said the Queen, cutting off her pleasurable flow of reminiscences.

"With great pleasure, Your Majesty."

Emma rose to her feet and approached the piano, while Cornélia opened a printed score. Soon the silence

---

1. Motto of the Order of the Garter, meaning "Evil to him who evil thinks."

was broken by the poignant notes of *Ah! non credea mirarti*, an aria sung by Amina, the heroine of Bellini's opera, *La sonnambula*. "Ah, you trust in your beauty, yet it is quickly forgotten…" Lady Erroll and Mrs. Rich listened, captivated. The music-loving monarch closed her eyes, humming occasionally, in a state of beatitude. At the end of the aria, the singer bowed low to the applause of the little group of spectators.

"We enjoyed it so very much," was the Queen's comment. "The Italian opera pleases us immensely. We once studied under Louis Lablache. Did you know that he sang at Beethoven's funeral in 1827? We also studied the piano under Felix Mendelssohn; it was at the beginning of our marriage to Albert. Our husband was determined that we be able to play music together. If you could have heard it! It was quite enchanting!"

She sighed and her tone changed.

"Let us hear something in a more popular vein now."

Emma chose to sing *Home, Sweet Home*. When she reached the lines "An exile from home, splendour dazzles in vain," her eyes filled with tears. She was almost overcome by an unstoppable emotion as she was transported back in time to her first recital after her mother's death. The begonias on the Queen's piano added to her attack of nostalgia: they had been her maternal grandmother's favourite flowers. While she sang, Emma relived the family holiday festivities in Chambly, hearing echoes of the joyous cries of her aunts, who were not much older than their two nieces, when the group would gather for afternoon tea. She thought of her grandmother cutting thick slices off a homemade loaf of bread, spreading them with a layer of fresh cream, and sprinkling them with maple sugar.

"You are weeping, my child," murmured Lady Erroll with solicitude when the song ended.

"The lyrics, written by the American actor, John Howard Payne, take me back to my own home, Madame," answered Emma.

"But the melody is English," said the Queen. "For us, it evokes the English hearth and home. Essentially the same for generations, they ensure the stability of our family life, just as the monarchy ensures the stability of the country. And now, sing Gounod's *Ave Maria* for us, my dear. We like that composer very much. Unfortunately, our mourning has prevented us from attending the London premiere of his opera, *Faust*."

Silence settled comfortably over the room. Then, once again, the angelic voice of the diva filled the air; it was a moment of eternal peace. The singer executed the hymn with expressive fervour through to the last phrase, *"in hora mortis nostrae, amen."*

Victoria's attention was unflagging, and the private recital continued with still more arias. Finally, the Queen congratulated the celebrated *cantatrice*, and asked her:

"You are of the Catholic faith, like all our French Canadian subjects, are you not? Yet I do not see any cross around your neck…"

Emma, embarrassed, lowered her head. Victoria got up.

"Our most heartfelt thanks for the delicious moments you have given us, Mesdemoiselles. A queen's life is often austere. Music applies a soothing balm to the sore wounds of our heart. You may leave us now. We wish you a safe return."

The two sisters curtsied gracefully and bade the assembly farewell.

In the cab, on the way back to the hotel, Emma said, "Did you notice that the Queen always speaks of herself in the plural? It will take me some time to get used to it! You may be sure, Nelly, that she will invite me again. And she'll go to hear me at Covent Garden, too."

"You're exaggerating! You know very well she never attends the opera or the theatre. You're dreaming if you think she'll really make an exception for you."

"What devotion to her husband! I should like to experience a passion like that," said Emma wistfully.

"You're joking, Emma! You must dedicate yourself to your career."

A few days later, a royal messenger delivered a small beribboned package to the Cavendish Hotel. Emma read the short note that came with it:

Windsor Castle.
July 8, 1874
Sir T.M. Biddulph presents his compliments to Miss Albani. Her Majesty the Queen would like her to accept this cross and this necklace as a souvenir of her visit to Windsor last week.

Under the wrapping paper was a jewel case containing a diamond-inlaid cross, to be worn as a pendant on a pearl necklace. With trembling hands and sparkling eyes, the singer attached it around her neck.

"I will wear it always," she whispered. "It will be my lucky piece."

The word "luck" drew Emma's thoughts to her belief that she had followed a predestined path. She visualized the crucial stages of this path, beginning with moments from her childhood. She remembered, evoking each scene in her mind.

2

"You'll be a musician, my child."

I was three years old when my mother gave me my first piano lesson. She had promised to teach me Beethoven's *Scottish Dance*.

"When you know it well, you can play it for Granny Rachel, " she told me.

I learned the piece very quickly, because I adored my maternal grandmother. She came from a Scottish family; her face was covered with freckles and she had a fiery temper. Although I loved the piano, I remember envying my little friends who could play in the garden while I practised indoors.

At about this time, our family moved to Plattsburgh in New York State. There wasn't enough

Emma Lajeunesse at five years of age.

Little Emma spent her holidays with her maternal grandparents near her childhood home on Rue Martel in Chambly.

work for Papa in Chambly. He taught harp and violin, while Maman gave singing lessons. She died in the United States after giving birth to my little sister, Mélina. The baby did not survive her for long.

When I was five, Papa became my teacher. I studied the piano according to the Bertini Method – playing and practising five hours a day! Papa thought it was the best way. He was proud of me, because in four months, I mastered all the thirty-five pieces of the Bertini course, even though my little fingers couldn't stretch a full octave.

Once I could read and write French adequately, I had a private classics tutor. My father was convinced it was necessary for me to learn Ancient Greek to develop my brain. The result of this was that I was accustomed to studying from an early age. "Brilliant" and "exceptional" were some of the comments that were made about me. Mr. Sexton, who had taught Greek in some of the great families of England before coming to North America, told Papa, "Your little Emma has an astonishing facility for Greek pronunciation; it will help her when she has to sing in several languages." This happened sooner than I could have imagined.

A six-and-a-half, I was singing arias from *Norma* and *La sonnambula* – "two operas by the Italian, Bellini, and among the most beautiful in the repertoire," according to Papa. By the time I was eight, I could sight-read music of any style and period.

People often criticized my father for driving me too hard, and for hitting me on the fingers with a rod when I mistook a note or lost the tempo. He only laughed at their reproaches. To him, I wasn't a child: I was a young artist who possessed exceptional gifts and whose duty it was to strive for perfection.

Cornélia, two years younger than I, also studied the piano. Our little brother, Adélard, a year younger than Nelly, was making remarkable progress on the violin. However, Papa was a lot less demanding of them than he was of me.

I'll always remember the month of April, 1856. I was eight, and it was not long after Maman's death. My father came to give me my daily harp lesson. I was absorbed in *Peau d'âne*, a Perrault fable.

"Emma, it's not the time to read: you must work on your technique now."

"Not today, Papa."

I didn't dare tell him that the index finger of my right hand was injured, and above all, I didn't want him to know the reason: I had hurt it while disobeying him.

"No lagging! Bring your harp!"

When I began to pluck the strings, my eyes filled with tears of pain. After a moment, my fingernail was torn off. I cried out and fainted, tumbling to the floor. Luckily, my father was quick enough to catch the heavy instrument; otherwise, it would have fallen onto my head.

I had hurt the finger by catching it in the back door of my aunt and uncle's house, hurrying in for supper. My father had gone to the United States to play the organ; I had been playing with my friends outside instead of practising and had forgotten the time. I had kept silent about the injury for fear of being punished when Papa returned home.

My vocation as an actress also came to me from the family: my maternal aunt Rose-Délima possessed a remarkable talent for inventing and telling stories. She changed her voice to impersonate each different character, enthralling us children. When I was still little, I too began acting out stories by gestures and mime, turning them into pure theatre.

Granny Rachel lived next door to us in Chambly. Her attic, filled with old dresses, hats, and purses, was a true Ali Baba's cave to us. We would dress up and perform musical dramas for our friends in the English section of Chambly – the "swells," as we called them among ourselves. I can still see myself draped in a cloth that served as an eastern costume, singing the soprano part in Félicien David's symphonic poem, *Le désert*. I sang perched on a rock made out of a wooden box, surrounded by my friends whom I had taught to sing the chorus.

Those were still the good times before my mother's death, when our lives were suddenly turned upside down. I believe Papa suffered more than the rest of us: he began drinking too much and became irritable – and even more strict with me! If I dozed off during my long practices, he would beat me. He had become obsessed with the idea of turning me into a prodigy who would conquer the world. I'm sure that if my mother had lived longer, she would never have let him adopt that excessive attitude towards me.

When Maman died, we returned to Canada to live with my aunt and uncle in Montreal, on the Rue Saint Charles Borromée. I felt uprooted there. Luckily for me, our neighbour, Madame Lavigne, took me under her wing. In the Lavigne's welcoming home, she reigned over no less than seven musicians! Her eldest boy, Arthur, wanted to become an impresario; Ernest, the second son, was a composer. He used to tell me that when I became famous, he would write songs for me. The youngest son, Émery, was studying to be a piano accompanist.[1]

I had become an accomplished musician and singer for a child my age. I was able to sustain high notes progressively longer. I was considered a phenomenon. My first public performance took place on September 15, 1856, in Montreal, at the Mechanics' Hall on St. James Street. I was awed by the large hall and the grandiose staircase; I still remember how small I felt. Before going on stage, I was terrified, but Papa was there to encourage me and give me confidence. Many times in my life, I was tempted to hold it against him for making my childhood so strenuous, but music and applause were always ample compensation for me and drove any resentment from my heart.

This first concert had come about through one of our visits to Mr. Seebold's store on Notre Dame Street. It stocked musical instruments and sheet music, and Papa and I went there so often that it was almost as familiar to me as our own home.

That day, I didn't want to go; I wanted to play at home. I was in my room combing my hair when Papa burst in, snatched the comb from my hand, and dragged me along with him. While Papa and Mr. Seebold were talking, I tried out a new piano in the

---

1. The three Lavigne brothers mentioned here all achieved notable success in the music world; Émery once accompanied actress Sarah Bernhardt on tour.

store. Mr. Crawford, a well-known impresario and a singer of Scottish ballads, came inside; he had been passing on the street, and hearing the piano, had been curious to know who was playing. "Emma is my daughter," Papa told him. "She sings well, too." I demonstrated, to Mr. Crawford's astonishment. Right then and there, he obtained my father's permission to organize a concert in which I would play the harp and the piano, and sing Scottish duets with him. I considered that I would have the perfect accent to sing these ballads, being of Scots descent on my mother's side.

    The recital was a triumph. A carpet of real flowers covered the stage; it was exquisite, but the scent was so overpowering that I almost fainted. In the programme, Mr. Crawford had included a few pieces that I had to sight-read and sing on the spot. One of them was *Cujus animam* from Rossini's oratorio, *Stabat Mater*. It was a challenge for me; I was nervous, but I succeeded well enough.

    That same season, my great-uncle Mignault, who was the priest in Chambly, organized a concert in my home town. I sang a French ballad, *Mère, tu n'es plus là*, and *Un ange, une femme inconnue*, one of my own compositions. Then I sang *Wenn die Schalben* in German, songs in Italian and Latin, some Scottish ballads, and finally, two English songs, *Home, Sweet Home* and *God Save the Queen* – the anthem that always concluded any public gathering. After that recital, I went on tour, to St. Jean, L'Assomption, Sorel, Joliette, Terrebonne, and Montreal.

    I was envied for my talent and success, but I would much rather have remained a little girl snuggled in my mother's arms in our modest home in Chambly. I can picture the house on Rue Martel: it had two stories and a gabled roof; the outer walls were covered by wooden shingles, and it looked onto the Chambly Basin. There was a white picket fence in the front yard, and magnificent lilac trees on each side of the house sent the most wonderful perfume wafting into my room in the month of May. There was a little garden at the back, surrounded by beautiful countryside with views of Fort Chambly and Mont St. Hilaire.

I remember the clattering of our shoes on the wooden sidewalk as we walked to church where my father played the organ at Sunday mass. Our childhood was immersed in a flowing river of music. In the evening, when we were in bed, we would fall asleep to the sound of Maman playing Chopin waltzes on the piano.

In the morning, delicious smells from my mother's dressing table floated through the air. To me, they evoked the music she had played the night before as we drifted off to sleep; intriguing emanations of violet-scented rice powder and almond-scented hand cream blended with whiffs of rose-milk and honey-water perfumed with mint, dill, or vanilla.

In September of 1858, the year I turned eleven, we were sent away to school. We were separated from my brother Adélard, who went to a boys' college. After spending our summer holidays at our grandmother's house, Cornélia and I left for the convent school in Sault-au-Récollet, on the north shore of the island of Montreal. Although I was now a boarder with the Sisters of the Sacred Heart, I still studied under my father: he taught music at the convent, which paid for our room and board there.

The Mother Superior of the convent, Mère Trincano, had soft black eyes, a smooth complexion, a perfect oval face, and fingers as slender as Maman's. This nun had dedicated her life to the strict education of young girls. She spoke against the new vogue of children's balls, imported from France, saying that they were "no more than vanity contests and little theatres of luxuriousness."

When we arrived, Mother Trincano took us on a tour of the school. We felt dwarfed by the huge corridors. We passed nuns escorting pupils who wore dark dresses with white cuffs and collars – the school uniform. In the library, a vast room with high, arched windows, I asked our guide if I would be able to read the books there. "Of course," she answered. "But we will decide which ones are appropriate for you at your age."

A wide stairway led to the dormitories. "This is your domain," Mother Trincano said, showing us two narrow cast-iron beds with white coverlets. Beside each bed was a washstand with a porcelain jug and basin on it. "For your Saturday morning bath, you will wash with your nightdresses on." We almost replied that this hadn't been the custom at our house.

The first nights that we slept at the convent, Cornélia wet her bed. I did my best to cover up these accidents, but it became impossible after a few days due to the smell, and soon, everyone realized what had happened. My poor little sister, humiliated and terrified, spent several days without speaking, and followed me about like a shadow.

Life at the convent suited me well enough, especially as I could play the piano and read my favourite books as much as I liked – including the stories of my beloved Comtesse de Ségur.

Music was my favourite subject. I was an exceptional pupil and won first prize every term in my first year. In my second year, I was barred from competition since I was on a much higher level than the other girls.

I even composed a hymn for Pope Pius IX and dedicated it to my great-uncle, the priest. I composed a triumphal march for my father, as a New Year's gift to him in 1860. That same year, on May 4, during a school recital, I sang another piece I had written, called *Les martyrs*. And on the occasion of Mother Trincano's birthday, I sang *Travail de reconnaissance*, which I had written for her. I became the star performer of the institution.

I experienced my first dramatic exaltation during a morality play that the school presented for Monseigneur Ignace Bourget, the Bishop of Montreal, who had come to officiate at our annual prize-giving ceremonies. Because I was not blessed with long blond hair like some of the other girls, I was not allowed to play an angel. I asked to play the role of the devil, who had to try to tempt Saint Anthony. The long-awaited day arrived. My hands were sweating and trembling as I waited in the wings for my cue. I hopped from one foot to the other, laughing and sobbing senselessly, wrinkling my black silk costume and fidgeting with my horned hood. My part was in the final sketch, which was intended to show the great piety of the saint as he prayed for strength to resist the Evil One's beguilements. But, instead of whispering to Anthony from over his shoulder, I began tickling his ears, pulling his hair, and shouting perfidious suggestions right into his face. The more the audience laughed, the more hysterical I became. Finally, the other students were obliged to drag me off the stage: I had lost all sense of reality.

The fever that had brought on this delirium lasted for three days. I remember hearing Mother Trincano saying to the doctor at my bedside: "The child is our most gifted music student; we would be terribly, terribly sorry to lose her."

Nelly and I continued to spend our summer holidays with our brother Adélard at my grandmother Rachel's house. I could play the piano and sing as long as I liked, or play with dolls with my girlish aunts.[1] Throughout the school year, the only games we were allowed were outdoor sports – our obligatory daily exercise. During the holidays, we went on country picnics. We dressed in the conventional style for the occasion: flounces, lace pantaloons, and strapped shoes for the girls, and a sailor suit for Adélard. And everyone wore straw bonnets or boaters.

Our aunts would come dressed in the same manner. We rode in uncovered carts, loaded with butterfly nets, hoops, tablecloths, blankets, and wicker baskets. The picnic lunch consisted of meat pasties, bread, ham, cold chicken, cakes, wild strawberries, and lemonade. A veritable feast!

After eating, we would run through the fields while the women embroidered or crocheted and gossiped and the men fished.

1. Emma once told an English newspaper reporter: "I never had a doll of my own."

In the evenings, my grandmother sang old Scottish ballads, accompanying herself on the piano. Occasionally, to make us laugh, she would bang down on the keys, making the begonias shake in their pot.

However, the holidays always ended too soon, and with them, the joyful romps in the countryside and the boat rides in the Chambly Basin.

That vision of carefree summer days seems to draw a curtain over my childhood memories. In August of that same summer of 1860, another stage of my life began, in which I would sing for a prince – my first crowned head.

3

One Day, My Prince Will Come

In the spring of 1860, a Montreal newspaper, *La Minerve*, announced: "The Prince of Wales will come to Montreal to dedicate the newly finished bridge, named Victoria, in honour of the Queen of England, his mother."

The Prince was indeed present at the opening ceremony on August 24; he screwed on the last bolt – a bolt fashioned of pure silver for the occasion. After this symbolic gesture, he was regaled by the four hundred voices of the Montreal Oratorio Society raised in a cantata. And I sang the soprano solo – I, Emma Lajeunesse, twelve years old. I must have looked very childish among all those gentlemen in

Emma arrived in Paris in 1868, at twenty-one years of age, to perfect her musical training and to launch her career as an operatic soprano.

their coats and tails and the ladies with their billowing crinolines.

During our rehearsals, I had heard a quantity of whispered gossip that I only half understood. It seemed that Prince Albert Edward, a handsome eighteen-year-old, was somewhat of a rake, a pleasure-seeker who frequently went to Paris for his diversions. That was why he was nicknamed "the Gallic Prince" and the "Prince of Romance."

A few days after the inauguration of the bridge, His Highness was scheduled to visit the Sacred Heart Convent! My father took advantage of the occasion to submit a petition, signed by more than fifty people, asking the Prince to write a letter of recommendation for me. This would help enormously to boost my career when I went to Europe, as Papa presumed I would.

Albert Edward's aide-de-camp, Major-General Bruce, refused diplomatically, explaining that, although my abilities as a child prodigy were unquestionable, I was still too young to hope for an engagement with any of the better-known musical ensembles across the Atlantic.

My father, undefeated, resolved to organize a benefit concert to cover the expense of European musical training for me. "Emma has nothing left to learn from me," he said. "She must study under the most reputable music teachers and she must have a scholarship to do it."

Papa worked tirelessly to put this project into action, while still teaching at the convent. I continued my own musical instruction with him. I was not always a model pupil, however; I liked playing tricks too much. There had to be some fun in my life, after all! In spite of this, I was turning into a well-behaved and accomplished young miss with my sights set on a spectacular career. My sister Cornélia was progressing too, following her own musical path.

Finally, on September 13, 1862, *La Minerve* advertised "a musical evening to assist the Lajeunesse sisters in financing their trip to Paris, where they will study at the Conservatoire."

The concert was held at the Mechanics' Hall in Montreal, under the auspices of the civil and military authorities. I performed on the piano and the harp and sang some of my compositions, accompanied by Nelly on the piano; my voice range was from mezzo-soprano to soprano in those songs. The next day, a newspaper reporter described my voice as that of "an exile from heaven." "We are proud," added the writer, "that this young woman is a daughter of our native land. We predict an international career for her."

Because of unwelcome interference from the Catholic Church, Papa was unable to gather the necessary funds. *L'Ordre*, the influential press organ of the clergy, had expressed the censorious opinion that "long voyages, particularly the wandering existence of performers, are pernicious. Emma Lajeunesse is known to be an innocent and pious soul: must we allow her to be exposed to this peril?"

My father was furious and considered emigrating back to the United States. However, one of his friends, the brilliant lawyer and politician Ludger Labelle, organized a benefit concert that drew a large number of music-lovers. Although the money raised was insufficient for our European plans, it did allow Cornélia and me to go to try our luck south of the border. We were obliged to leave our cherished convent to go into the wide world; it was the only alternative if we wanted to go further in music.

Thus, the following year, Papa, Cornélia, and I found ourselves in Saratoga Springs, an elegant watering hole for the rich in upper New York State. It was in the United States that our hopes were realized and my career took off in a definite manner. The American public was fascinated by "the young prima donna" named Emma Lajeunesse.

As soon as we settled in, a concert was organized at Rand's Hall, with Cornélia as my accompanist. The hall was packed. My programme included arias by Rossini and Verdi, *The Last Rose of Summer* (the beautiful Irish song arranged by Sigismond Thalberg), and an aria from the romantic opera, *Martha*, by Friedrich von Flotow. The comments published the next morning in the *Troy Daily Times* were eloquent: "She warbles with the perfect naturalness of a bird."

In Albany, not far from Saratoga, I sang at a military gala attended by State Governor Sydney, several senators, and a crowd of four thousand spectators.

In Johnstown, fifty miles northwest of Albany, Cornélia and I performed together at a charity benefit: we both played the piano and sang duets, Nelly in her charming contralto voice. Each of us was given a star-shaped brooch, with wishes that we would become equally brilliant stars!

Soon after, at the consecration of Albany's new bishop, John J. Conroy, I sang Johann Hummel's motet,[1] *Alma Virgo*.

We remained in Albany, where I became first soprano soloist at St. Joseph's, Bishop Conroy's church. It was there that I learned to sing masses by Mozart, Cherubini, and Beethoven. The church administrators had found a good thing: I was young – and therefore cost them very little – and I sang beautifully in Latin, Italian, German, French, Russian, and English, as well as in the Irish and Scottish styles. Moreover, I could play the organ, and the one at St. Joseph's was considered the second best in the whole country. I was really too slight for this colossal instrument, but I managed well enough. I also directed the church choir and composed music for it! I carried out these duties at St. Joseph's until 1868; it was an ideal training ground that helped me become one of the most appreciated oratorio singers in England many years later. The Catholic churchgoers of Albany took me to their hearts. When the altar of a new chapel was consecrated in January 1867, they came in huge numbers to hear me sing.

On that occasion, Maurice Strakosch,[2] the impresario from New York City, was present. He had come to Albany with Pasquale Brignoli, the tenor who had sung the role of Alfredo when Verdi's *La traviata* was introduced to the American public in 1856. Meeting

1. Motet: a religious choral composition, not using words from the liturgy. Johann Hummel (1778-1837) studied with Mozart and developed the first piano method with a rational treatment of fingering.
2. Brother-in-law of the opera diva, Adelina Patti.

my father, they told him: "Your daughter has the voice of an angel. She possesses a rare talent and genius."

This inspired Papa to approach Bishop Conroy and express his fervent wish that something be done to obtain the financial means for me to study music in Europe. The Bishop agreed, and entrusted the organization of two benefit concerts to the wife of a well-known Albany notary.

The music-loving prelate was in the audience for the second of these concerts, together with all the notables of the capital, all of them brimming with pride for "*their* girl from Albany." Quebec had never seemed so far away! I recall my father's voice, swelling with emotion as he announced to the cheering audience that after many years of struggle, his daughter could finally leave for Europe to study with the best teachers obtainable.

The notary's wife presented us with gifts and a cheque for three hundred dollars; it was the first time my father had ever seen such a sum. This amount, added to our savings, was enough for my great departure, after nine years of hopes and disappointments. I was twenty-one but still looked like an adolescent due to my extreme slimness.

A young man named David Turner, whom I had noticed several times at concerts and receptions, was not put off by my childlike appearance. He asked to meet me, together with Cornélia, at a tearoom. I was wary of his intentions, and pleading a headache, stayed at home. I asked Nelly to go without me and to apologize for my indisposition, which she was only too willing to do.

Mr. Turner tried to hide his disappointment from my sister, but in spite of his good manners, he couldn't stop talking about me throughout their *tête-à-tête*. Nelly was taken aback when he declared that he had two passions in life: music, and Emma Lajeunesse.

He repeated his invitation to me. In the end, I agreed to go for a walk with him along the bank of the Hudson. He confessed his love for me and begged me to marry him. He told me that he was an amateur violinist and had formed a chamber music group with his friends; he promised that he would share my love of music if I were his wife. However, nothing he said could make me waver in my firm resolve to pursue my career abroad.

A second request for my hand was forthcoming, this time from an older, well-established Albany factory-owner, who offered me a comfortable life. I turned down this proposal as well, for the same reason that I had refused the more attractive Mr. Turner.

The rejected businessman was not entirely disheartened: "I am sorry, as I am very much in love with you. However, I will donate to your scholarship fund, in the hope that you will allow me to visit you in Paris."

"I am most grateful," I replied, "and will look forward to seeing you there."

I fully believed Papa when he said: "It would be absurd for you to become the wife of a rich industrialist when you are only interested in singing. You're not made for marriage." Cornélia's view was the opposite: "You're mad, Emma! He's a wonderful man who would have made you happy and given you security. I would have accepted in a minute!"

I felt no regret over my decision. I told one of my friends: "I have a feeling inside that must be expressed; something more that I must accomplish. I cannot resist the urge."

By the end of 1868, I was ready to embark for Europe. Cornélia was to accompany me; even though the money we had raised was not enough for her to continue her own studies, it was unthinkable that a well-brought-up young lady should travel alone. Besides, Nelly was happy and excited at the prospect of coming along. We crossed the Atlantic to Southampton aboard the *Great Eastern*, a steamer of twenty-one thousand tons with a huge propeller and two gigantic paddle wheels. As soon as we were on board, a fellow passenger treated us to a harrowing account of the ship's previous crossing: there had been a storm so violent that the cattle in the hold had broken out of their pens and had erupted into the dining saloon where the first-class passengers were eating dinner!

My greatest fear, however, was that we should arrive in England on the thirteenth of the month, or on a Friday, which would have been a bad omen for the start of my European adventure. We reached *terra firma* without any untoward incidents, and soon after, we left for France. We carried a letter of introduction from Bishop Conroy, addressed to the Sisters of the Sacred Heart in Paris, and asking them to help us find respectable lodgings in the city. In spite of the Bishop's kind effort, the nuns were clearly mistrustful: we were from North America – could we still be good Catholics? They sent us to a pension that proved unsuitable. After a few days, we did find a congenial home in Paris, thanks to a young pianist whom we had met by chance.

And what a home! We stayed with the Baroness de Laffitte, a banker's widow. The banker – her second husband – had squandered most of his fortune by dabbling in politics, and his widow was obliged to take in boarders to maintain the style of living she was accustomed to. We were surprised to discover that, even though the house was lavishly decorated and furnished, there were no sanitary facilities of the type we had on the other side of the ocean! We had to put a good face on it and eventually got used to this minor inconvenience.

Madame de Laffitte welcomed us warmly. Thank heaven she was an opera-lover! I have never forgotten the moment when she told us that her first husband had been Jean-Blaise Martin, a noted French singer; his name had been given to a particular register in which the lighter head tone is prominent: the *baryton Martin*.[1] She added: "When Jean-Blaise was going to sing in the evening, he would have a very light meal in the afternoon and wouldn't use his voice again for the rest of the day. Also, he would go to bed early the night before a concert. I advise you to adopt this regime if you want to have a successful career."

The Baroness then asked me to sing for her, and declared herself won over. She pledged her support and friendship, and she proved it several times over, starting with the time I contracted typhoid fever. I

---

1. A register between baritone and tenor; the term is not in use today. When Debussy's opera *Pelléas et Mélisande* was first performed (in 1902), the role of Pelléas was sung by Jean Périer, a "baryton Martin."

must have eaten or drunk contaminated food or water and had not taken the proper precautions; without Madame de Laffitte's care, I probably would have died.

Our kind landlady did much to advance my career, introducing me to many of the eminent figures of the Parisian musical milieu, like Prince Poniatowski, a singer and composer who had studied under Rossini and had remained his friend, and the directors of the Opéra, the Opéra-Comique, and the Théâtre Italien.

Madame made sure that I frequented both the opera and the theatre. She also arranged for me to receive an invitation to a ball at Les Tuileries given by the Empress Eugénie; it was a thrilling occasion for me.

Through this whirl of social events, I did not neglect my musical instruction – although my first singing lesson with Maître Gilbert-Louis Duprez, the retired tenor and composer,[1] was a disaster.

I arrived late, quite out of breath, at Maître Duprez' luxurious studio. I was naturally in awe of this man whose reputation was formidable.

"You are not on time," he rapped out, without even a *bonjour*.

"My humblest apologies, Maître," I stammered.

"There is no possible excuse for it, Mademoiselle. Put the fee for your lesson in the lacquer box on the piano and come back at the right time next week."

I paid the money and went out, hiding my tears.

The following week, my lesson seemed to be going well, until he stopped me in mid-song.

1. Duprez was the first tenor known to have sung high C from the chest.

"Your Gilda in *Rigoletto* is execrable. Your Marguerite in *Faust* is worthless. For the love of heaven, do not close your throat when you sing the high notes. Your technique is abominable; you are incapable of modulating your phrasing. Sing high C and hold it."

I took a deep breath, and the note came out pure and sweet.

"Not bad. Do it again but hold it longer this time."

I did what he said, holding the note as long as I could, until it petered out in a *glissando*.

"You must breathe more deeply," he advised, placing his hand on my abdomen. "You must strengthen your diaphragm. If you wish to become a *grande cantatrice*, you will have to work, work, work!"

Feigning not to notice my dismay, he added in a fatherly tone: "Just as much as technique, you must refine your sensibility. All art has its source in human vulnerability, but keep your tears for the arias in which you are required to express emotion."

"Maître, I have worked to develop my voice since my early childhood, but I feel as if I were starting from the beginning again."

"Go ahead, control every breath you take," he continued, without acknowledging my remark. "Concentrate on your voice, and eat only what is good for it: lean meat, fish, boiled vegetables, and toast. Only satisfy your appetite after you have given a successful performance; that will be your reward!"

"I couldn't. I would faint from hunger!"

"Keep active eight hours a day and sleep nine hours a night: you will soon feel the difference. Even your soul will sing! You have a good light soprano voice, but it lacks ripeness."

I had imagined that I was free of a hard taskmaster when I left my father's tutelage, but Maître Duprez was even more exacting. I realized that to him, I was not a child prodigy, but simply a student like any other.

I carefully noted all his advice and criticism. Among his many bits of wisdom, I particularly remember his saying: "There is no better method of voice training than singing scales and doing exercises using the feminine syllables. Each note must be sung with equal resonance; each syllable must be pronounced with its own particular recitative value."

I believe that my teacher was gradually won over by my determination, although he was miserly with his compliments. There was a small private theatre near his school where he allowed his more advanced pupils to perform. My first appearance there was as Marguerite in the garden scene in *Faust*; and the audience applauded enthusiastically. I treasure the memory of finally hearing my teacher's praise: "She has a beautiful voice and possesses the sacred flame; she is of the wood from which great flutes are fashioned."

At the same time, I took classes in sacred music from François Benoist, one of the best organists in Paris – another necessary string in my bow, I thought. Duprez, however, advised me to concentrate on operatic singing. "You are a born nightingale," he told me.

Paris was the loveliest place on earth to me in those youthful days. I expressed this opinion to a Canadian acquaintance who had been touring the Continent. He concurred, but gently reproved me, saying: "Emma, you move in a very worldly circle here in Paris. You live in the midst of great reconstruction projects, right beside Charles Garnier's new opera house, the new Place de l'Étoile, and the *grand boulevards* with their cafés and theatres. You see nothing of the crisis brewing among the working classes. Strikes are breaking out and are being crushed by the army. The Parti Républicain is gaining influence at the expense of Napoléon III, who is old and ill. There is the foreign threat, too: Bismarck is working to create a united and strongly armed Germany, primed for war."

"But isn't the French army as powerful?" I asked, surprised by his serious tone.

"Powerful, and too sure of itself, besides. I would even say belligerent, but with an arsenal as outdated as its strategies. France has no allies; a military conflict would be fatal. My dear Emma, you must go to Italy at your earliest opportunity."

Prince Poniatowski agreed with this advice, but from a musician's point of view. He offered to commend me to the best-known Italian singing teacher, Signor Francesco Lamperti of Milan. "For anyone wishing to rise to the top in the opera, I recommend the Italian method. It produces a magnificent quality of voice. Singers trained in France tend to sing through their noses instead of their throats. Vowels are the basis of the Italian method. Just compare the words *amore* and *amour*, *vita* and *vie*. Italy is the natural homeland of song."

The Prince was a friend of Maurice Strakosch who had heard me sing in Albany, and who had become the most important opera impresario of the day. Mr.

Strakosch was in Paris and accompanied the Prince to a recital that I gave one evening. He paid me a lovely compliment: "Your voice has matured since Albany: it is richer and fuller. And what elegance of tone!"

By this time, my dear Maître Duprez was in ill health and could not keep on all of his students. That was another reason for my decision to move after those heady months of life in Paris. However, I was distraught at leaving this stimulating milieu, and afraid of leaping into the unknown. Thank goodness Nelly was going with me! The Baroness kindly organized a benefit concert that enabled us to set off with enough funds to tide us over on our arrival in Milan.

Town of Chambly, Albani Archives.

Emma as Tamara in *The Demon* by Anton Rubinstein at Covent Garden Theatre in 1881.

Town of Chambly, Albani Archives.

Emma as Marguerite in *Faust* by Charles Gounod at Covent Garden Theatre (London) in 1875.

4

In the Land of Bel Canto

Maestro Francesco Lamperti always told his new pupils: "If you adopt my method one hundred per cent, you will be able to sing anything."

Once again, I had to bend my will to a strict and critical disciplinarian. Lamperti refused to teach any members of the aristocracy, because, according to him, they tended to regard singing as a diverting accomplishment rather than as a serious career. He once disparaged a dilettante by saying: "She sings like a countess."

Prince Poniatowski visited Milan a few months after I had been with Maestro Lamperti and came to evaluate my progress.

"Her trill is faulty," he remarked to Lamperti.

"It will fall into place, my friend," answered the maestro. "She is like a bottle of effervescent water: one has only to uncork her and everything gushes out. Moreover, I am writing a treatise on the trill which I will dedicate to her."

For the first few lessons, Maestro Lamperti concentrated on the syntax of vocal music that all great singers must master: breathing, voice projection, nuance, and phrasing.

I was also instructed on how to strengthen my diaphragm by bending my waist as far as possible to each side, then backward and forward – as far as my corset would allow, that is!

"… seven, eight, nine…" Lamperti called out rhythmically. "Keep going, up to twenty!"

"But I'm exhausted and very hungry!" I protested.

"*Madonna mia!* There are still two hours left until lunch, Emmina! Lie on your back now."

I lay down on the carpet. The professor placed a pair of heavy volumes on my abdomen.

"This will strengthen your diaphragm," he explained, adding yet another large book to the pile. "Lift the books – with your stomach muscles, not by arching your back."

At first, I thought I would never manage it. My vision began to blur with the effort.

"Loosen up, my dear! Do your relaxation exercises. Breathe; breathe again. You must train yourself to lift the books ten times. When you succeed in doing it easily, we will pass on to the next step. Only after you master it, I will have you sing an aria."

I accepted his severe regime, dreaming all the while that it was the key that would allow me, the *petite Canadienne*, to send my voice resonating back to the very last row of seats at La Scala.

Cornélia and I became increasingly fond of life in the northern Italian metropolis, although it was too full of temptations for our meagre means. My immediate goal was to obtain a singing engagement. Several impresarios and owners of concert halls who frequented Lamperti's studio had offered me roles. However, the maestro had his own plan for me: "You will make your debut in Messina. The opera house is small, but the Sicilians are the most difficult to please among opera-lovers."

In the little apartment we had found in Milan, it was not easy for me to practise my vocalises. Cornélia would be bent over the piano, almost fainting in the hot, closed air of the apartment, with its odour of simmering spaghetti sauce. Our only window looked on to a narrow courtyard; we could not open it often, as several rooms that gave on to the courtyard were occupied by other music students, and they had to practise too.

One day, I stepped onto the tiny balcony outside our window for a breath of fresh air, and a joyous impulse made me launch into *O sole mio*. Window after window popped open, and when I finished, I was treated to clamorous applause and demands for an encore! A flower seller below took some roses from his cart and threw me a bouquet.

Just at that moment, there was a knock at the door. It was Signor Lamperti. He had come personally to announce that my engagement for the winter opera season in Messina had been confirmed; the only thing needed was my signature on the contract. "You will begin this summer, in a pre-season production, but your real debut will be in December, as Amina in *La sonnambula*, by Bellini. You remember, of course, that the composer was a native of Sicily; you must be worthy of his memory and rise to the occasion."

I was overjoyed; my most sanguine hopes had been realized. My career would be launched by performing the principal role in a major work by the most romantic of Italian composers. Besides, I knew that Bellini was born on my birthday, All Saints' Day, and I believed it was a favourable omen for me.

My teacher brought me back down to earth by reminding me that all of Bellini's arias are exceedingly difficult to sing. "*La sonnambula* requires great vocal prowess and an infinite amount of wind, especially for the *aria della follía*. However, we have worked together for nine months now, and your technique is extraordinarily good for such a young singer. You are ready, Emmina! Throw your whole heart into winning over the public. You must become Amina and the character will live through you. If you can carry off this role, you are capable of any soprano role in the repertoire and your career is made."

That evening, I changed my last name. We had heard comments that the name Lajeunesse did not roll of the tongue as musically as it should in the land of bel canto. Among the pseudonyms suggested, I chose Albani: it was the name of a patrician Italian family whose members were all dead, except for one ancient Cardinal. It was also my tribute to the city of Albany,

International Star

where I had been given the opportunity to spread my wings and set off on my career.

The distance between Milan and Messina is more than 1000 kilometres. Nelly and I made the entire journey in an exceedingly slow train, without stopping anywhere along the way. However, we were compensated for our discomfort by being able to contemplate this marvellous country from north to south.

From the deck of the large steamer that ferried us across the Straits of Messina, we saw our destination nestled at the foot of the Peloritani Hills. The city's streets were aligned with the coastline fringed by cerulean waters. We were billeted with a friend of Maestro Lamperti's: a Sicilian duchess, who, like Baroness de Laffitte, rented out rooms in her home to make ends meet.

I was impatient to arrive at the opera house. During the first rehearsal of *Un ballo in maschera* at the imposing Teatro Vittorio Emmanuele, the conductor halted the musicians to tell me: "My child, your success is assured, and will be grandiose."

A few days after Christmas, 1869, it was the night of our first performance of *La sonnambula*. I was alone onstage, facing the darkened hall and an unpredictable audience that would either acclaim me or shower me with ridicule. I felt a moment of panic. Then, the silence was broken by the orchestra striking up the first bars of the opera. I began to sing – me, the little girl from Chambly, before a large crowd of sophisticated European opera-lovers – and in a foreign language, *their* language. When the final notes of the last scene were played, I knew that I had triumphed. I was given fifteen curtain calls!

The next morning, a critic wrote in the *Gazzetta di Messina*: "The audience was so surprised and fascinated that the theatre seemed to have been transformed into a cage of raving madmen, if one is to judge by the shouts, the applause, and the curtain calls. Mademoiselle Albani wept tears of joy."

I wrote a long letter to Papa in which I entreated him to join us in Messina to share our happiness. "It is the great launch of my career, and I still need your advice if I want to reach the top. You will see: from our windows, we look out at the coast of mainland Italy; it is breathtaking."

As the season went on, my success increased, as did the compliments and tributes paid me. One afternoon, I received an enormous package containing valuable jewellery. The sender, rendered ecstatic by my performances, had offered me his wife's most prized adornments! They were immediately returned, of course. Another day, an old, almost blind man asked to meet me. He said that he had never heard anyone sing Amina as I did. He owned an orange grove, and every time he came to hear me sing, he had a basket brought to my dressing room, filled with oranges, each one wrapped in silk! On the night of my last performance, he asked me if he could pass his hands over my face, to be able to picture me in his mind.

I received several marriage proposals in Messina. My photograph hung in the windows of all the shops. People imitated my hairstyle and the way I dressed. I had become an idol almost overnight!

My happiness was complete when I heard Cornélia exclaim, "Papa is coming!" as she waved a letter from him in her hand. A few weeks later, Nelly and I escorted our father from the ferryboat to our Sicilian palazzo. He admired everything, from the pink and apricot-painted buildings to the proud peasants and artisans with their large-wheeled carts gaily painted with legends from the Crusades and drawn by little ponies caparisoned with ostrich plumes, pompoms, and tinkling bells. "Albani," he repeated, bemused. "I'll never get used to it!" But his face glowed when passers-by greeted us with cries of *"Brava, l'Albani!"*

That day, the Duchessa de Cipriani had invited a few guests for tea and was waiting for us in the garden, amid flowering citrus trees and exotic flora that gave off intoxicating scents. Papa bent low and gallantly kissed the hand of our noble hostess. I remember her face, surrounded by silver curls, and her clothes – the customary outfit of an aristocratic Sicilian widow – black silk gown, black gloves, black fan and black parasol, and a watch fob from which hung a delicate silver timepiece. She was immensely proud of her fluency in French.

Before removing to his hotel, Papa visited our quarters: a big square room with three long windows. He exclaimed over the *trompe-l'oeil* mural paintings that created the illusion of pilasters, marble balustrades, and flower-filled urns against a background of flitting, round-cheeked cherubs. He gazed at the inevitable religious subject gracing the ceiling: it was the Virgin Mary ascending towards a deep blue heaven that teemed with gravity-defying, acrobatic angels holding flowers and doves. He was also given a tour of the ground floor, where a vast dining room was decorated with murals representing the bloodiest scenes from the opera, guaranteed to kill the appetites of any guests who were not opera fanatics.

My father's greatest surprise was when we took him to mass on Sunday morning. Nelly and I knew what to expect: in Sicily, it is the custom to introduce opera melodies into the sacred liturgy. For example, in the Eucharist, when the priest brings the chalice of holy wine to his lips, the aria *Infelice, il veleno bevesti!*[1] from Donizetti's opera, *Lucrezia Borgia*, might be sung. Only the Italians have such an audacious sense of humour!

Papa soon left Messina for Florence; he was travelling ahead of us so that he would have ample time to explore that city.

Before we left to join Papa, the countess lent us her barouche and her coachman so that we could travel down the coast to Acireale, near Catania, where Bellini was born in 1801. I was to sing at the gala opening of the Teatro Vincenzo Bellini. The landscape between Messina and Acireale was striking, with its bare mountain slopes, sheer rock faces and shadowy ravines. This lunar landscape, drier than bones left in the sun, was occasionally relieved by silvery olive trees, refreshing valleys, sweet-smelling orange groves, and pale golden beaches.

Acireale was a good-sized seaport. I was treated like a diva on my arrival there. I was given an official welcome by the local dignitaries, and Cornélia and I were lodged in a venerable palazzo that had been

1. Woe! You have drunk the poison!

refurbished especially for our stay. On one side, we had a view of the menacing volcano Mount Etna, while on the other, we looked out onto the sea. The best families of Acireale sent us wine, fruit, meat, and poultry, and the nuns from the local convent sent us cakes and sweetmeats.

As the dramatic heroine of *La sonnambula*, I attracted music-lovers from Catania, Syracuse, and even from distant Palermo. The critics praised me lavishly. "Who is this Albani?" queried Signor Bertolani in *Il Corriere Siciliano*. "This question will no longer be asked in coming years: Emma Albani is an exceptional creature in whom the woman and the artist attain equal perfection; in whom the singer and the actress vibrate in unison. It is impossible to say whether she is more remarkable by the brilliance of her genius or by her strength of mind, the finesse of her ideas, her perfect pitch or her roundness of melody. Her voice is made to fill the hearts of those who are capable of finding consolation for human misery in art. This singer from across the Atlantic has perfectly understood the Italian art of bel canto."

On the evening of my benefit night,[1] I was showered with flowers and jewellery.

We left Sicily with regret. I sang for a short season at Cento, a town near Bologna, the city of arcades that resembles a stage set from a Molière play. Here, I sang the role of Gilda in Verdi's *Rigoletto* for the first time. The audience insisted on encores of Gilda's aria, *Caro*

1. Benefit nights were given by opera stars at the end of the scheduled performances; the singer was allowed to keep all the proceeds of the performance and also received valuable gifts of appreciation.

nome, of one of the duets, and of the quartet, *Bella figlia d'amore*. Admirers from Bologna presented me with so many large bouquets that they had to be transported on donkeys! The combined scent of all these blossoms was overpowering: I was afflicted by a migraine headache and was forced to abruptly leave the stage.

In Florence, crowds of people awaited me: Maestro Lamperti had proclaimed to the inhabitants of the city that Emma Albani was "the most accomplished musician and the singer with the most perfect style who has ever emerged from my studio."

The Teatro Politeama in Florence was an outdoor amphitheatre; only the stage was covered. Even a driving rain did not dampen the audience's enthusiasm, and they remained spellbound under their umbrellas. Fortunately, it was the month of July, and very warm! We sang right through the downpour. My performance as Adèle in Rossini's *Le comte Ory* and my signature role of *La sonnambula* won me the accolade of having "a silver voice."

Jenny Lind, "the Swedish nightingale," was in Florence; she had retired from the stage to dedicate herself to teaching. When she came to congratulate me in my dressing-room, I was overcome with emotion.

Beside the jewels I received, which included a diamond brooch and earrings, I was given an immense laurel wreath of beaten gold. Luckily, my benefit nights had made up for the relatively low amount that I earned for my performances.

Nelly and I, escorted by Papa, spent a delightful time discovering Florence, the city of art. We visited the Uffici Gallery and haunted the Ponte Vecchio, exploring the goldsmiths' and leather-goods shops. I found inspiration for many of my costumes and accessories there.[1]

Another delightful surprise in Florence was the news that I was engaged to sing in Malta for the five-month winter season of 1870-1871.

The charming island of Malta in the southern Mediterranean had belonged to Great Britain since the beginning of the century and was the most important base in the world for the British fleet. The opera house was in the Maltese capital of Valletta. This city had been fortified by the Knights of St. John, one of the religious and military orders from the era of the Crusades; the Knights had moved to Malta from Rhodes and had defended the island against the Turks in the sixteenth century.

On the billboards, my name, in bold letters, appeared opposite the roles that I would sing in Malta: Amina in *La sonnambula*; Rosina in Rossini's *Il barbiere di Siviglia*; Lady Harriet in *Martha* by Von Flotow; the title role in Donizetti's *Lucia di Lammermoor*; and Isabella in *Robert le diable* by Giacomo Meyerbeer. In addition, I had to sing the role of Inès in Meyerbeer's *L'Africaine*, at very short notice: I had only two days to master it after the young woman who was to sing the role suddenly fell ill.

As a supplement to the programme, the audience, many of whom were from the British Isles, called on me to sing *Home, Sweet Home* and *The Last Rose of*

1. Opera singers were responsible for their own stage outfits; Emma Albani visited museums so that she could create costumes with an air of historical authenticity.

Summer. I found it strange that a *Canadienne* was indulging their nostalgia for their homeland! On the evening of my farewell performance in Malta, a poem composed by the officers of the Royal Navy was brought to me by a dove!

A few of the higher-ranked English officers made attempts to woo me. One of them did attract me but Cornélia reminded me of my duty. "It would be all right for me to allow myself to be courted, but not you with your responsibilities," she chided.

Apart from my besotted admirers, I made some good friends on the island, including the Governor, Sir Patrick Grant, and Sir Cooper and Lady Francis Key. At one the receptions given for me, I met Colonel McCrea, who urged me to try my luck in London. He interceded with one of his friends, the impresario James Henry Mapleson, who wrote to invite me to join his Italian opera troupe at Her Majesty's Theatre.

I was eager to try my luck in the English capital, but first, I had a last engagement in Acireale, this time at a charity benefit for the victims of an earthquake that had hit the city. When we left Valletta, Colonel McCrea ordered the navy gunboats to line up for a processional salute as our steamer made its way out of the harbour. "An exceptional tribute," I thought, too affected to speak.

5

Happy Days in Europe

To reach London in June of 1871, we were obliged to travel north through the entire Italian peninsula, just as the country was undergoing the final throes of the struggle for unification. General Giuseppe Garibaldi, fighting in the name of King Vittorio Emmanuele II, had finally taken Rome, which had been defended in vain by the Papal Zouaves. Some of the Zouaves had been dispatched from France and counted several French Canadians among them. Now, Garibaldi's red, white, and green ensign fluttered over the Eternal City, replacing the white and gold banners of the Holy Father, who had shut himself up inside the Vatican palace.

Frederick Gye, manager of the Royal Italian Opera at Covent Garden, engaged Emma Albani in 1871; she performed the greatest opera roles there until 1886.

International Star

There had also been turmoil in France during our absence. The empire that we had left was now a republic. We learned what had happened from fellow travellers as we made our way towards the English Channel: in July 1870, Emperor Louis Napoléon III had declared war against Prussia, provoking an attack on French soil by the vastly superior German forces. The Emperor was made prisoner, was deposed, then fled to England with the Empress Eugénie and their son. Paris, besieged and starving, had resisted the invasion. France was obliged to sign a humiliating peace treaty, but that did not end the troubles. Civil war ravaged Paris when the popular front known as the Paris Commune was savagely suppressed.

How peaceful London was after Paris! Thirty-five years into Victoria's reign, the city was impressive with its stately buildings and its green commons and parks with their flowering shade trees, winding paths, and gay bandstands.

The day after our arrival, Nelly and I set out for our meeting with James Henry Mapleson of Her Majesty's Theatre. Our hired cab stopped in front of an elegant theatre. I gave my name and asked to see the manager. While we waited in a large anteroom, a secretary approached and told us that his employer had not been expecting us. Disconcerted, I took out the letter I had received in Malta, care of Colonel McCrea. The young man went off to make further inquiries, and Cornélia and I were left feeling ill at ease. Perhaps there had been a mistake: were we in the right place? Could the cabman have misunderstood me?

There was a piano in the room, and to make us forget our nervousness, Nelly sat down at the bench and struck up the first chords of *Casta diva* from Bellini's *Norma*, drawing me into the music and inspiring me to sing. In the midst of the aria, I became aware that someone was watching me: a corpulent, distinguished-looking gentleman of a certain age was standing in the doorway. He had unobtrusively come to listen. He saw that I had noticed him, but gestured to me to continue singing. When I had finished, I turned to him, somewhat embarrassed.

"Congratulations, Mademoiselle," he said. "You have a magnificent voice. But why are you here?"

I took out my letter and held it out to him. He read it quickly and burst out laughing.

"But you have come to the Royal Italian Opera at Covent Garden! The most important opera house in London! I am the manager. Allow me to introduce myself: Frederick Gye, at your service."

Both Nelly and I were rendered speechless by this revelation, and were even more astonished when the gallant Mr. Gye immediately followed it up by a proposal:

"I would like to engage you, Miss Albani. I was looking for a light soprano.[1] I'll speak with the other administrators, and if they agree, I can offer you an exclusive contract – for the next summer season, with the possibility of extending it for five years. Can you come back here tomorrow at ten?"

I stammered: "Next summer... do you... does that mean April, 1872?"

---

1. Today, this kind of singing voice is referred to as a coloratura soprano.

"Until then, we will find you some roles that are not in our prima donnas' repertoire at present. You'll have plenty of time to work on them."

In the face of Mr. Gye's forceful manner, there was nothing for it but to acquiesce. I reflected that my visit to his competitor, Mapleson, would have to be put off until some future date.

"My secretary will be happy to show you around our establishment, my dears," Mr. Gye ended peremptorily. He bowed, turned on his heel, and left the room.

We admired the ornate gilt banisters of the monumental stairway, the lustrous woodwork, and the marble busts of musicians lining each side of the lobby.

When we left the theatre, an evening fog had descended. Through the thick mist, we could barely distinguish the flowers, fruit, and vegetables on the stalls of Covent Garden Market. Behind us, gas lamps threw their eerie light on the opera house, making it seem like something out of a dream. At that moment, I had a vision of myself inside the building as *La sonnambula*, tiny under the huge red curtains being hauled up above the world's most renowned stage, and as other heroines still unknown to me and whom I would have the joy of discovering.

I signed my contract a few days later. Mr. Gye advised me not to go about town too much. "Lie low and avoid being seen at social events. That way, when you debut at the beginning of the season, you will burst onto the scene like an apparition."

His advice was unnecessary, since Maestro Lamperti had invited us to stay at his summer residence on Lake Como, where he would help me prepare for my engagement for the short winter season in Florence.

Before our departure for Italy, Nelly and I had some free time to visit the art galleries of London, and, more importantly, to attend the opera, where some of the greatest singers of the day were performing. Thus, we heard the Italian-American singer, Adelina Patti, the reigning operatic soprano at that time. We were enchanted by Pauline Lucca, who sang Inès in Meyerbeer's *L'Africaine*; to me, she was a model by her vocal artistry, her unique way of expressing emotion, and by her acting skill. There was also Miss Caroline Miolan-Carvalho, who particularly impressed me in the Jewel Song from *Faust*; her grace, her phrasing, and her tempo were all so perfect that I burst into tears.

When we arrived in the town of Como, Maestro Lamperti told me that he found me even more beautiful and elegant than when he had last seen me. It may have been because of my pastel-hued silk dress, and the fact that I now wore my hair in a chignon with a little fringe that emphasized the oval shape of my face. I was happy, and was made even more so by the serene beauty of the lake ringed by the snow-covered Italian Alps.

As I spoke several languages, I was able to converse with all the maestro's friends and pupils. Lamperti coached me in the parts that I was scheduled to sing in Florence that winter: Adèle in Rossini's *Le comte Ory*, and the title role of *Mignon*, a recent work by Ambroise Thomas. Mignon is a mezzo-soprano role, but as my range was wide, I could sing in this register without straining my voice, and without endangering my ability to slip back into the higher register.

International Star

I prevailed upon Lamperti to obtain an introduction for me to Thomas, who was then the director of the Conservatoire de musique in Paris. At sixty, he was considered the greatest living composer of the era. The meeting was arranged and I made a short trip to the French capital. The composer welcomed me kindly and gave me some precious advice on how to sing Mignon; thus, I would be sure to interpret the role as faithfully as possible. "It is not just a matter of singing and breathing, of nuances and voice projection," he told me. "The meaning of the lyrics is of prime importance." He convinced me to sing one of the recitatives while laughing, an idea that never would have occurred to me.

In Florence, I sang *Mignon* nine times in ten days. The director of the Teatro della Pergola, where we performed, wanted me to extend my contract, but Mr. Gye, advised by telegram, replied that the London opera season had begun, and I was required there. My heart beat faster when I received this summons.

∽

London at last! The opera season in the capital is sacred to British music-lovers, who are among the most demanding in the world. Besides that, sitting in the audience for my English debut performance would be my most implacable critic: Papa.

The director of the Royal Italian Opera at Covent Garden had his own peculiar strategy for stimulating interest in the season's programme. In accordance with the proverb, "Good wine needs no bush," he considered it vulgar to advertise his star performers. A stark and simple announcement was released to the press: "Miss Albani, the remarkable young soprano, will appear in Italian opera at Covent Garden under the management of Mr. Frederick Gye."

I brought a trump of my own to this strategic London debut: although I was twenty-four years old, I still looked much younger.

The atmosphere at Covent Garden was not so exuberant as in Italy; preparations for the performances were made with military precision. Everything was carefully planned to go off without a hitch, but even so, I was much more jittery than in Messina, Florence, or Malta. I was aware that I was about to play my most important card.

On opening night, Mr. Gye knocked on my dressing room door. He was impeccably dressed in a black tailcoat and cravat. I thought at first that he had brought me flowers, in keeping with the established custom, but he simply asked me:

"How do you feel, my dear?"

I answered that my throat felt so constricted that I was sure I would not be able to sing a note.

"You'll be marvellous, I'm quite sure. Now, I'll stay with you for the next ten minutes, and you'll sing to me alone."

He sat at the piano and began to play the grand aria from *La sonnambula*. After refreshing my throat with spring water from a crystal spray-bottle, I threw my whole heart and soul into the first phrases of *Ah! non credea mirarti*.

"Ten minutes, Miss Albani!" cried the stage-manager, tapping on the door. In a daze, I went to take my place on stage. I knew that Mr. Gye would be sitting in the first box on the right, between my father and Cornélia. When the curtain rose, I glanced at them and resolved that I would sing only for them.

I saw hundreds of pairs of opera glasses being raised so that their owners could get a good look at the new songstress. My first high notes seemed weak and stilted to my ears, but as the performance proceeded, I felt my strength returning, buoyed by my father's attentive presence. My voice grew in amplitude, rich and crystalline right up until the last note, which was drowned out by thunderous applause.

An enormous bouquet of white roses awaited me in my dressing room; the message that accompanied the flowers was simple but gratifying: "I placed my confidence in you, and I was not mistaken. Welcome to our new diva. The Director, Covent Garden."

The reviews in the London newspapers were unanimously laudatory. The critic of the *Musical Times* wrote: "The great event of the month has been the success of Mlle. Albani, who made her début as Amina in *La sonnambula*. With a genuine soprano voice, and a remarkable power of *sostenuto* in the higher part of her register, this young vocalist at once secured the good opinion of her audience. She progressively affirmed her authority throughout the opera until the final '*Ah! non giunge*,' her brilliant rendering of which produced a storm of applause that could only be appeased by her appearing three times before the curtain."

Over the subsequent weeks, Cornélia clipped out all the reviews about me and sent them to Papa, who had returned to Canada. We also occasionally sent him gifts of money. I was happy to be able to make life a little easier for my first mentor in this way; I owed him so much more! As I still needed his musical coaching, as well as someone to help me administer the business aspects of my career, I wrote to ask him to come to live with us in London for a few years.

During my first season at Covent Garden, I gradually gained confidence. I was delighted at having won over the English opera buffs, who gave me noisy ovations instead of clapping with the ends of their fingers as they usually did. I was especially elated when I heard myself being compared to Patti, Grisi, and Miolan-Carvalho.

To reassure myself that these compliments were not utterly fantastic, I asked Nelly to attend performances to observe those divas, after which she could offer me her judgment and critical comments. During this period, I was hard at work, preparing to sing the title roles of Donizetti's *Lucia di Lammermoor* and Linda di Chamounix, Lady Harriet in Von Flotow's *Martha*, and Gilda in *Rigoletto*.

One afternoon, when I was practising my vocalises in our rooms, a visitor announced himself with the words, "Miss Albani, I presume?"

As I immediately guessed, it was Henry Stanley, the New York newspaperman whose name was renowned throughout England for his exploit of tracking down the Scottish-born explorer, David Livingstone, in the heart of Africa. Mr. Stanley was staying next door to us and wanted to write a piece about me for the papers! He was an exceedingly charming fellow, but was the kind of person who never stays for long in one place. In any case, my heart and mind were fully occupied with other matters!

My traditional benefit night surpassed all expectations, although an unfortunate incident almost marred the evening for me. An over-enthusiastic admirer threw me a bouquet attached to a jewel box, which hit me hard on the forehead. I was obliged to leave the stage, holding my head with one hand and clutching the awkward offering in the other. My pain was somewhat eased, however, when I saw the pretty diadem inside the case.

The same evening, I received another package, this one in my dressing room. The box, sheathed in blue velvet, held another diadem: of diamonds! The card was signed Ernest Gye. "The director's son…" commented Cornélia, eyeing it. She added in an ironical tone, "Mademoiselle has made an impression."

Following this set of performances, I received proposals to sing at some of the great English festivals and at the Théâtre Italien in Paris. The director of that theatre, whom I had met at Madame Laffitte's establishment years before, engaged me to sing in *La sonnambula*, *Lucia di Lammermoor*, and *Rigoletto* for the 1872-1873 opera season.

The Parisian critics, writing of my coming French debut, seemed prejudiced against me. One comment was: "She is neither a great beauty, nor does she possess Patti's piquant charm…"

On the opening night of *La sonnambula*, my first European teacher, Gilbert-Louis Duprez, was in the audience. He came backstage after the performance and enfolded me in his arms, uttering warm congratulations.

He had brought me a photograph of himself, signed "From Duprez to Albani."

Not everyone in Paris shared his enthusiasm: the reviews were mixed, which hurt my feelings considerably. While one journalist wrote that "a new star has appeared on the horizon of the opera," another one, in *La France*, opined, in what I thought was a glaring example of French chauvinism, that "Mademoiselle Albani is like an Englishwoman: she wants to bring out all her good points at once, doing too much, too well. In spite of her brave spirit, the ragged-edged timbre of her voice betrays the fatigue of practising. Her performance smacks of the schoolroom: she is merely a distinguished talent, well-versed and efficient, but her voice does not rise to any great heights of lyricism and is not always on key."

Fortunately, Frederick Gye, who had travelled to Paris for the occasion, was there to apply a balm to my wounded pride. He took Cornélia and me out to supper at the chic Café Anglais, and reminded me, "Lucia is an enormously demanding role, one of the most difficult in the repertoire."

I was very glad to return to London, where I was on conquered territory. In my second season at Covent Garden, I sang Catherine in *Les diamants de la couronne* by Auber,[1] Ophelia in Ambroise Thomas' *Hamlet*, and the Countess Almaviva in Mozart's *Le nozze di Figaro*.

My father and Nelly paid close attention to what the public and the newspapers said about me. Excerpts

---

1. Daniel François Auber, French composer (1782-1871).

from reviews included comments such as: "Her *mezza-voce* is of a rare beauty. She recalls Jenny Lind, who excelled in half-tones. Her charm and delicacy create an irresistible atmosphere;" "In *Rigoletto*, Albani has succeeded in conveying the poetry of Verdi's masterpiece, the libretto of which was inspired by Victor Hugo's historico-tragical drama, *Le roi s'amuse*;" "The success of Miss Albani's return is not diminished by the fact that she is already known to us. Ovations of this kind for so young a performer are rare in London. Only Miss Patti, whom Miss Albani appears to rival in both talent and popularity, could have won such accolades."

Although, inevitably, we were rivals for many years, Adelina Patti and I were friends. She herself told me the following anecdote: "I was walking with my husband in Regent Street, and we paused to look at some photographs in a store window; yours was one of them. Two men came up behind us, and one of them commented: 'There's the portrait of Albani. They say she'll cut Patti out.' I turned around and said to him: '*Thank you*, sir!'"

One evening, after a performance, I was delighted to see Colonel McCrea, home from Malta with his wife. He smiled from under his bushy white mustache, asking me: "Wasn't I right to advise you to try your luck in London?"

Another visit was less joyful – that of the Empress Eugénie, dressed in widow's weeds. She was mourning Napoléon III, who had died in early January. She told me that her dear friend Victoria was also grieving for her departed spouse (although Albert had been dead now for a dozen years), and had invited her to the Côte d'Azur. The Queen of England owned a little villa at Cap Martin, hidden behind the mimosa trees, umbrella pines, and date palms of the Mediterranean coast. The locals often had glimpses of Victoria, unaccompanied, driving a buggy drawn by little Irish ponies.

We heard of David Livingstone's death – not in the African bush, but in his bed in London. His friend, Henry Stanley, was at his side until the end. I thought fondly of Stanley, my charming erstwhile neighbour, and wondered if I would ever have the opportunity to travel to Africa. Perhaps one of the cities of that continent possessed an opera house, and one day, I would be invited to sing there.

I did receive an invitation to sing soon after that, but in a very white, very cold land. Cornélia packed our trunks full of warm winter clothing: we were to leave for Russia, where I would be the star of the opera season in the imperial theatres of Moscow and St. Petersburg. I faced the daunting challenge of succeeding Adelina Patti in the hearts of the fanatical Russian opera lovers. The invitation had come directly from Tsar Alexander II himself.

6

A Disturbing Character: the Tsar

"The Russian winter is just like our Canadian winter!" I affirmed.

Cornélia agreed, adding:

"This strange white light on the snow banks takes me right back to Chambly – it makes me feel very homesick."

It was December, 1873. We had just arrived in Moscow.

My sister and I, covered by bear rugs, were comfortably installed in a troika, gliding through the city streets. The three trotting horses pulling the arabesque-shaped sleigh rhythmically jingled the bells on their harnesses. Nelly exclaimed over the neo-classical

Town of Chambly, Albani Archives.

Albani in the role of Elisabeth in the 1876 English premiere of *Tannhäuser* by Richard Wagner, at Covent Garden.

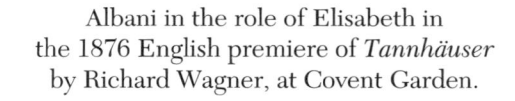

Town of Chambly, Albani Archives.

Albani, circa 1878.

façades of the public buildings, the huge bazaars, and the elegant houses. Bundled forms with only their eyes uncovered darted about busily, emerging from or vanishing into dark little side streets. Suddenly, the troika brought us into a vast open space, and the enormous mass of the Kremlin and St. Basil's Cathedral rose before our eyes. It was stunning.

"I have heard that there are also many smaller churches, filled with icons and incense – where one can hear the Orthodox liturgy sung by priests with astonishing *basso profundo* voices," I said.

"You're so romantic," my sister chided me. "In this cold, my only thought is for a warm fire of maple logs and the smell of boiling tea!"

By evoking this reminder of our childhood, Nelly had turned us back into the Lajeunesse sisters of Chambly, Quebec.

The previous evening, however, at a gala given by Prince Dolgorouky, Moscow's governor, I had been one hundred per cent Albani, gracefully at ease amidst the official honours rendered me, and the opulence of the great Muscovite families.

We had given nine performances in Moscow's opera house, of *La sonnambula*, *Lucia di Lammermoor*, *Hamlet*, and *Rigoletto*. Tsar Alexander had been remarkable by his absence, although the splendid two-headed golden eagles mounted above the empty imperial box had been a constant reminder of the grandeur of his absolute power.

Our tour continued in St. Petersburg, the Russian cultural capital and the sovereign's winter residence. The opera season would begin following the traditional

New Year's Day reception held by the Tsar in the Winter Palace, to which our troupe was invited. The closing part of the soirée took place outside the palace, with His Imperial Majesty's ceremonial blessing of the Neva River, to the acclamations of the guests, officers of the guard, and the populace.

Later, I excitedly told Cornélia the details of what I had seen during that memorable evening.

"Imagine, caviar served with a soup ladle – a pure gold ladle! The court of Napoléon III is nothing compared to the Russian one!"

"Bless me, I was forgetting," said my sister sarcastically, "Mademoiselle has also danced at Les Tuileries, at the court ball reigned over by the beautiful Eugénie, Empress of France."

"If you had could have seen the Tsarina Maria's diamond collar," I continued, undaunted, "and the silver-gilt goblets filled with Imperial Tokay, the Tsar's own special Hungarian vintage!"

Rehearsals, as well as the actual performances, were carried out in the most professional manner. It is true that the opera houses of Moscow and St. Petersburg had no equivalent in Europe: much attention was paid to the singers, who had to protect their voices from the rigours of the Russian winter. All the local *artistes* were employees of the Imperial House. They had fabulous costumes and stage sets, as well as excellent technical support, at their disposal. This made it possible for them to stage unique, colossal productions. Compared to these theatres, the Paris Opéra seemed like a small town hall.

The capital itself resembled a huge opera house: the palaces were painted in pastels that were reflected in the freezing waters of the Neva; the numerous canals spanned by elegant bridges had given St. Petersburg the epithet of the Venice of the North. Citizens of consequence, dressed in gay finery, strolled along the long avenues, greeting each other and exchanging courtesies. Humbler men and women from the four corners of the Russian Empire wore the bright traditional clothing of their respective regions; bearded ecclesiastics strode about in long robes, their hair flowing onto their shoulders. Students promenaded in their uniforms, and European ambassadors and their wives flaunted the latest styles of Paris, London, or Berlin. But all these paled before the mounted Cossacks of the Imperial Guard, glowering, silent fellows wrapped in thick military cloaks and coiffed in enormous fur hats, who always held their spears at the ready, alert to the slightest threat to their master. The Tsar was well protected.

His Imperial Majesty attended every one of our performances. The repertoire was the same as the one we had presented in Moscow.

One performance stands out sharply in my memory: I was singing Gilda in *Rigoletto*. When I went onstage, I was struggling against my usual jitters and the horrible fear that I would be incapable of singing a note. One technique I used to suppress my sense of panic was to concentrate on a particular point in the audience, and that night, I fixed on the Tsar's box, as if I were going to sing exclusively for him. I took a deep breath and moved forward under the house lights. The orchestra conductor raised his hand discreetly and the music began. When I finished *Caro nome*, I experienced the pleasure of a few seconds of absolute silence that was finally broken by the tumultuous roar of the audience, on their feet applauding. The curtain rose and fell a full twenty times that night! By the end of it, I was trembling with joy, under the bouquets that rained down from almost all of the boxes.

Dizzy from the undiminished clamour, I went back to the tranquil oasis of my dressing room, where tea with honey was kept hot for me on a samovar. I changed from my stage costume into a creamy-white satin *peignoir* bordered in white fox.

There was a knock at the door. An officer announced that, as an exceptional honour, the Tsar had invited the company to be received in the Imperial box, which was large enough to serve as a salon where he sat with his court favourites.

Alexander II was enthroned on an elevated dais. I had changed my clothes so quickly at this unexpected summons that my corset was pinching me; as a result, my curtsey was lopsided. This made the Emperor smile. I had a close-up view of a balding man in his late fifties, with mutton chop whiskers and voluminous dyed mustachios. He looked rather like a hibernating bear, although his square jaw and his penetrating eyes had an undeniable appeal. His voice, in any case, was irresistible. He spoke French and English fluently.

He held all of my attention, making me temporarily unaware of the crystal lamps whose light bounced off the ladies' jewellery and the gentlemen's military decorations.

The Tsar rose, came towards me, and handed me a gift: it was a portrait of himself in oils, in a diamond-inlaid frame. I'm afraid my mouth fell open in surprise.

After that tribute, I summoned all the skill I possessed to be the best Ophelia ever heard. After the *aria della follía*, I was given thirty curtain calls! The Tsar mounted the stage, an exceptional gesture on his part, and spoke to me:

"Mademoiselle Albani, you are spellbinding! Your voice is as clear as the snows of our Mother Russia. You have a Russian soul; I recognize you as one of us."

"My home is also a land of snow, Sire."

"Yes, I know that Canada is almost as vast as my empire. Tell me about the songs of your country."

For a long moment, he kept me apart from the rest of the company, speaking to me about music with deep emotion.

Every evening, I experienced anew the deep joy of singing for this man who was a contradictory combination of strength and goodness, haughtiness and benevolent simplicity.

I also felt the public's vibrant response when they heard me. The stage around me was always littered with flowers and little beribboned packages containing gifts. But the Tsar had already given me the best of them all: a splendid set of diamond jewellery that included a crucifix.

For my last encore in my performances in St. Petersburg, I had prepared a popular Russian song. The stagehands would roll out a piano and I would accompany myself in *Matouvschia*. I usually had to sing it over and over again as the audience belted out the chorus. When I left the theatre, invariably a crowd of male students would be waiting outside and would run alongside my troika as it took me to my hotel.

Towards the end of January, an exceptional event interrupted the course of the opera season: the Tsar's only daughter, Grand Duchess Marie Alexandrovna, was to marry Alfred, Duke of Edinburgh, Queen Victoria's second son. Victoria herself was coming to St. Petersburg with her suite to attend the wedding.

No expense was spared to make the ceremony truly impressive. Our company was charged with interpreting hymns of joy during the wedding banquet.[1] There, I saw Victoria, at her most regal and dignified, for the first time.

The opera season went back into full swing right after the wedding. When the curtain had fallen after our farewell performance, the Tsar came onstage to thank us. He was followed by court attendants, and valets carrying trays that held goblets of Veuve Cliquot champagne. "To the health of the most beautiful and most marvellous of divas," proclaimed the sovereign, raising his glass and bowing to me. In this manner, I was consecrated as the ruling *cantatrice* of the Russian Imperial Court.

To the other members of our troupe, he presented gold, silver, and gilt medallions stamped with his likeness, the clasps embellished with rhinestones, strass, or diamonds.

To me, he gave a magnificent solitaire diamond ring. He took me aside to slip it onto my finger, and stood for a long moment, looking down at my hand in his. He drew his face closer to mine, and made an astonishing declaration: "Madame, since the day that I

---

1. Emma would sing at several royal weddings after this one.

attended the opera in London with the Prince of Wales and the Shah of Persia, you have occupied all my thoughts. Have you not been aware of it?"

"I am only an *artiste*, Sire. I cannot believe that Your Majesty could be interested in me other than as a performer."

"But you are also a queen, Madame – a queen of the vocal art."

The champagne and the emotions aroused by this unexpected declaration gave me the fleeting impression that an exquisite spell had been cast on me. Was I in an opera, or was this reality? Was I Violetta in a meeting with Alfredo? I could almost hear the strains of *La traviata* resonating in my heart. I quickly pulled myself together in the same way that I did before a performance: I took a deep breath that slowed my thudding heart, and was able to respond in a calm, slightly distant manner.

I reflected that my gallant admirer was, after all, one of the Romanoffs, known to be a hot-blooded dynasty. Since my arrival in Russia, I had heard many tales about the supreme ruler of the empire. People took it for granted that Alexander's charm, omnipotence, and incalculable wealth allowed him to obtain anything he wanted: the most luxurious palaces, the most spirited horses, and the most beautiful women.

Cornélia, of course, had warned me, saying, "The Tsar will do everything he can to seduce you. Keep in mind that you would be neither the first nor the last opera singer to become a prize for his trophy room."

I didn't dare tell Nelly that I was deeply attracted by this man – not by the all-powerful autocrat, but by the thoughtful and attentive music-lover, the aspect of himself that he had revealed to me.

My main preoccupation at the end of our Russian tour, in mid-February, 1874, was whether my benefit night would go off well. We greatly depended on the money collected at these special performances; many other valuable gifts besides money were included in this largesse.

Cornélia and I were selecting the arias and the Russian songs that I would perform at the benefit concert when the Chief of the Hussars was announced. Colonel Sergei Youssoupov had come with an invitation from the Tsar. "His Imperial Majesty has charged me to tell you that you are expected at the Palace for supper tomorrow evening after the performance."

I answered that I was gratified by the invitation but was undeserving of such an honour and needed a little time before deciding whether to accept it.

That night, my sleep was disturbed over and over again as wild dreams alternated with periods of wakeful anxiety. I felt that I had become Amina, sleepwalking on a narrow path between unbridled yearnings and self-discipline.

In one of my dreams, I was onstage. I had just finished singing and was bathing in the warmth of the acclamations of the public. The Tsar was standing beside me, not in his usual military regalia, but dressed as Boris Godunov, the hero of Mussorgsky's opera that I had seen in rehearsal. "Come," he said. "Everything is ready. The consecrated *cantatrice* of the Imperial House cannot refuse her Tsar a celebration of her success in the very site of her triumph."

International Star

The stage, as well as the boxes and rows of seats, were suddenly empty of people. The stage decor recreated the Duke of Mantua's palace in *Rigoletto*. A spotlight illuminated a royal feast in the centre of the stage; a table was garnished with silver candelabra, fine porcelain, crystal goblets, vases of flowers, and ice buckets containing bottles of Veuve Cliquot! Alexander stood, singing as he poured out the champagne, letting it froth over the rims of the goblets. He tapped the tip of a silver dagger onto a glass, producing a high C. A valet answered this signal by rolling in a trolley covered with caviar, smoked fish, and *blinis*.[1] Another servant brought a capon stuffed with truffles, and a chocolate whipped pudding. The Emperor took my hand.

"Nothing is too good for you, my precious. This theatre belongs to you now; you may sing any role that you choose. Stay in Russia with me. You shall be my queen and the refuge of my heart!"

I struggled to resist his urgings and answered, "Sire, the court overflows with beautiful princesses at your beck and call."

The Tsar begged me to call him Alexei as his intimates did.

The scene was magically transformed into the winter night; I was in a troika with Alexander, covered in sables. We were gliding through the deserted streets of St. Petersburg under the hazy yellow light of gas lamps. Soft, wet snowflakes were falling. I felt naked under the furs. Alexei took me in his arms. Suddenly,

---

1. Thin Russian pancakes.

Cornélia's disapproving face loomed over us, and I cried out to her, "I love the Tsar, and he adores me!"

She answered in a regretful tone: "I knew this would happen! Don't forget, you are not the first, and you won't be the last!"

At that point, I woke up. As I emerged from that muddled state between dream and reality, one clear thought stood out in my mind: *My sister is right. I have only to ask and he would give me a villa and an allowance. But I would be only one among many... do I really want to be a mistress, a kind of sub-tsarina, while now I reign over the opera world?* Ah, non, merci!

However, doubts still assailed me: how much longer would my success last? I loved St. Petersburg and the surrounding countryside – it reminded me of Quebec. I felt at home. Should I go or stay? I was infatuated with the Tsar; he had broken down my defences. In spite of that, I still preferred my music and my freedom.

Cornélia, seeing that I was awake, asked, "Emma, *chérie*, have you decided about the Tsar's invitation?"

"Yes, I have, Nelly. I will inform His Imperial Highness that I am very touched by the favour he has shown me, but work must take precedence over pleasure."

My benefit night in St. Petersburg brought in everything I had hoped for, and more. The most beautiful gift I received was a butterfly made of an emerald surrounded by rubies and diamonds, worth eighty thousand gold francs![1] With this, not only could I pay

1. More than four thousand U.S. dollars at the time.

my debts, but I could finance my brother Adélard's studies at the seminary. Above all, I could purchase a house for my father's old age – the house that he would call "Villa Albani."

"You are very generous to Papa," remarked my sister. "Yet you have said that he robbed you of your childhood."

"Yes," I admitted, "but isn't it thanks to him that Emma Lajeunesse is now Albani?"

Albani, the first time she sang the role of Elsa in Wagner's *Lohengrin*, at the New York Academy of Music, in 1874.

7

Travelling the Paths of Glory

Emma emerged from her reverie. "So much has happened since then," she mused. "What would have become of me if I had succumbed to the Tsar's charm?"

"But what a silly thought! The Queen has honoured me with her friendship, I'm in London, and time is pressing." The 1874-1875 opera season was a very busy one for Albani: she had a heavy schedule of performances at Covent Garden and at the Liverpool Festival. She would also go on her first American tour: to New York City, Albany, back to New York City, then to Boston, Philadelphia, Baltimore, Washington, Cincinnati, St. Louis, Chicago, and Indianapolis. Her travelling companions would include her faithful Cornélia, and Ernest Gye, acting as his father's agent in the United States.

The Lajeunesse girls did not travel lightly. Emma reminded her sister, "You know how cold it can get in October; we can't cover up too much." Accordingly, Nelly filled their stylish Vuitton trunks with layers of cloaks and capes, raincoats, scarves, muffs and kid gloves, as well as an assortment of flowery hats – it wouldn't do to go about bareheaded. To this, she added day dresses and evening gowns. On the large transatlantic steamers, it was not uncommon for upper-deck passengers to change their clothes as often as four times a day, and on this crossing, the young songstress and her companions were travelling first class.

The ship passed close to the Statue of Liberty as it moved into New York harbour. On the pier, a clutch of newspapermen were waiting for Albani, who disembarked in a grey dress augmented by a bustle, a blue-grey jacket that matched her eyes, and a frivolous velvet-ribboned hat. This lovely vision declared to the press: "I only eat a little and I rarely go out. A certain discipline is necessary if I want my voice to keep its clear timbre."

The façade of the New York Academy of Music, at the corner of 14th Street and Irving Place, was plastered with posters announcing Albani's coming performances in *Lucia di Lammermoor*, *Rigoletto*, *Mignon*, and *La sonnambula*. Emma's impresario, Max Strakosch – the brother of Maurice, whom she had met in Albany – was as pleased as punch: the shows were all sold out, presaging the success of the important New York leg of the Albani tour. The public was not disappointed by the diva. The *New York Herald Tribune*, the morning after Emma's first performance, was unequivocal in its praise:

"The Academy of Music has rarely been the scene of such a genuine triumph as the one obtained by Miss Albani last night."

After this success, Emma felt more confident when she set off for Albany, her adoptive American home. She was welcomed as a prodigal daughter by the proud townspeople. In the words of the *Albany Argus*, "Now she returns, every hand is extended to welcome her back home."

"Nelly," asked her sister, "You remember Miss Bulger of the Sacred Heart Convent in Kenwood, don't you? She's written a poem for me! She has joined the order as a nun. We must go and visit her."

Soon, rumours began to circulate in Albany that Emma was engaged to be married. When these wild conjectures reached the ears of the person concerned, she acted quickly to dispel them, and the following day, the *Albany Morning Express* issued a rebuttal: "Miss Albani's admirers will be pleased to know that, in spite of her remarkable success, Miss Emma remains heart and fancy free, just as she was on the morning she left her home on Arbor Hill six years ago."

When Emma returned to New York City to sing *Mignon*, an unexpected development awaited her. Her impresario asked her if she could replace a sick colleague in a new role. She would have fifteen days in which to learn the music and lyrics.

"It's the main soprano part in Wagner's *Lohengrin*," Max Strakosch told her. "Elsa is a great role. You'll sing in Italian, but your familiarity with German will be an advantage: you'll be able to convey the essence of the Teutonic soul."

Albani's immediate and instinctive reaction was to accept the challenge.

At the hotel, Ernest Gye, who had remained in Manhattan during her triumphant visit to Albany, asked her, "Do you really think you should take on such a modern work?"

"I'll dedicate all my time to it," she answered in a tone that brooked no argument.

Perfecting the role of Elsa at such short notice would be a considerable feat. Emma reflected that if she had taken more time to consider the proposal, she probably would have turned it down. She fretted over her commitment, but kept her worries to herself.

The opening night of the opera arrived all too soon. Emma was rehearsing at the last minute, alone, pacing up and down in her dressing room. She knelt (she never sang sitting down when she was wearing a corset), humming to herself. After a moment, she rose, donned a full-length brocade robe and unpinned her hair, letting it flow onto her shoulders. Albani was now Elsa. She straightened her back, lifted her chin, and squeezed the cross pendant, Queen Victoria's gift, in her left hand. It was time to go on stage.

"Even Wagner's detractors must admit that his harmonious melodies exercise a peculiar fascination. Miss Albani acts and sings as if she were the high priestess of Wagnerian opera," wrote a critic in the *Republic* of November 26, the day after Emma's first *Lohengrin*.

Albani had always had courage; now that she had acquired self-confidence, nothing could hold her back.

In Philadelphia, she received a letter from her father, telling her that a biography of her, written by Napoléon Legendre[1] had just been published. Emma was touched by this tribute, although she hadn't yet forgiven her native country for not having given her more recognition in the early days, when she had really needed it.

The tour was due to end in Indianapolis, but Albani's success was so great that Max Strakosch went ahead and scheduled extra performances.

"But Max, ever since I started at Covent Garden, I've never sung two days in a row. Mr. Gye insists upon it, as you very well know," Emma said, annoyed.

"I thought that in the circumstances, you would accept. It's a flattering compliment to you and a boost for your career," answered the flustered Mr. Strakosch. "I've already booked the dates."

That was too much. "Without consulting me? You'll just have to replace me, or cancel the performances." Turning to Ernest Gye, the diva added: "Next time we go on tour, I want everything clearly stipulated beforehand. In writing!"

In February 1875, Albani and company travelled eastward to New York, where the ship for England was docked. Sitting together in the train, they exchanged their impressions of the tour. Emma declared:

"I confess that I prefer Europe to North America. It's more a civilized continent. I fit in there. But for

1. Napoléon Legendre was a poet and journalist, and a founding member of the Royal Society of Canada.

nothing in the world would I act like those British expatriates who create little Englands wherever they go, especially in the colonies, where they conceive it their duty to govern defeated peoples according to their own standards."

"Their attitude of conquering heroes oppresses people everywhere," agreed Cornélia readily.

"However," countered Emma firmly, "for my part, I am proud to be a British subject."

Ernest nodded approvingly at this, while Cornélia pressed her lips together.

An invitation awaited Albani upon her return to the English capital: to sing *Lucia di Lammermoor* at the Teatro della Fenice in Venice, opposite Francesco Tamagno, a rising young tenor. Emma hadn't met him, but she knew of his reputation as a seducer of women.

"He may be a wonderful singer, but if he makes any comments about my décolleté, I will simply ignore him. He's only twenty-three, after all, and has a lot to learn. Who do these hot-blooded Latin singers think they are?" scoffed Emma, still in her twenties herself.

In Venice, all went smoothly. Tamagno acted with unexpected reserve towards his leading lady.

"I believe they have exaggerated about him," said Emma to her sister in their hotel room.

"Ah, but you've become an ice maiden since our return from Russia," Cornélia needled her.

"Touché!" acknowledged Emma's ruefully.

The window of their Venice hotel room gave on to the Grand Canal. Emma wrote to her father:

Dearest Papa,

My thoughts are of you as I look out at this sublime city with its pink palaces, its byzantine domes, and its canals. Last night, I sang before King Vittorio Emmanuele and Queen Margherita, who wore nine ropes of pearls. Magnificent! Emperor Franz-Josef was also present; it was his first visit here since the cession of Lombardy to Italy. Unfortunately, his beautiful wife Elisabeth – the famous Sissi – did not accompany him; she must be travelling elsewhere.

When I left the theatre, to my great amusement, I stepped into the canal instead of into the launch! They fished me out very quickly, thank goodness. Gondolas escorted me to my hotel, where I was serenaded. It was marvellous! Cornélia sends her love.

In London, spring had arrived. Daffodil shoots were pushing up through the earth, people threw open their windows, and the clopping of horses blended with the sound of trundling carriage wheels.

Albani was at home, honing the roles she was to perform at Covent Garden, including Marguerite in *Faust* and the Countess Almaviva in *Le nozze di Figaro*. In *Rigoletto*, Signor Francesco Graziani was to sing the title role of the jester. "The English adore him," complained Albani, "but they don't realize how difficult it is to work with him. When his back is to the audience, he makes jokes at the most dramatic moments and it takes a superhuman effort to keep a straight face!"

In May, Albani was Elsa in the English premiere of *Lohengrin*; in keeping with Covent Garden tradition, the work was sung in Italian. Emma had insisted on performing it, despite Frederick Gye's fears that the British public would find Wagner too forbidding. With her fine musical instinct, Emma realized that the German composer was ushering in a completely new style. Among other Wagnerian innovations, she appreciated his inventive use of *leitmotif* to reinforce the dramatic significance of the opera's themes and characters.

Albani plunged deeply into the study of her Wagnerian roles – Elsa in *Lohengrin* and Elisabeth in *Tannhäuser*, which was scheduled to open in London the following season. She was helped in this by Franz Wüllner, conductor of the Munich opera house orchestra and one of Wagner's close friends. While in Munich, Emma fell under the spell of the city's great parks, the half-timbered Bavarian houses, and the town hall with its façade of animated figures that come alive to mark the hour.

The director of Covent Garden was indeed taking a risk by including Wagner in the season's programme, but his audacity was well rewarded. The production was a wild success. It didn't hurt that the stage sets were grandiose and the entire performance outstanding from an artistic point of view. Albani was obliged to sing Elsa's prayer over and over again before the audience would allow the opera to continue. Hans von Bülow, another well-known Wagnerian conductor and a pupil of Franz Liszt, declared, "If Miss Albani comes to perform in Germany, she'll show the Germans how Wagner can be sung!"

International Star

In September, at the beginning of the English festival season, Albani was asked to perform a quite different repertoire from that of grand opera: at the Norwich Festival, she sang a choral work by Mendelssohn, *Hymn of Praise*, and created[1] a cantata composed by her friend, Sir Julius Benedict: *The Legend of St. Cecilia*.

The autumn festivals in England are triennial, except for the Preston Festival, which only takes place every two decades. The residents of the host towns and regions look forward to these events and turn themselves inside out to be hospitable. Parties of festival-goers throng to the churches and cathedrals where concerts of sacred music are performed; profane works figure much less frequently on festival programmes. Banners are hung and period costumes are worn, creating a truly festive atmosphere, which continues for a whole week.[2]

Albani rounded off her professional activities in 1875 by a tour of England and Ireland. In Dublin one evening, her hotel was surrounded by six thousand people, who refused to disperse until she had sung *The Last Rose of Summer* from her balcony.

In 1876, the London critics expressed golden opinions of Albani's interpretation of Elisabeth in *Tannhäuser*. That same year, when Queen Victoria was consecrated Empress of India, her subjects in the great

---

1. Singers and musicians "create" a work when they perform it in public for the first time.
2. Over her career, one of Albani's most popular successes at the English festivals was her rendering of *Angels, Ever Bright and Fair* from Handel's oratorio, *Theodora*.

95

subcontinent saluted the mythical British Empire as incarnated in her small, dumpy person.

Albani was in increasing demand. The entire season's programme of the Théâtre Italien in Paris revolved around her; she sang her ever-successful favourite roles, in *Rigoletto*, *La sonnambula*, and *Lucia di Lammermoor*. She also sang Elvira in *I puritani*, another well-loved Bellini opera, and Zerlina in Mozart's *Don Giovanni*. All of this was a sweet victory over the xenophobia she felt she had encountered during her Parisian debut eight years before.

"Nelly, please ask the chambermaid to lay out my most beautiful gown for tonight," Emma ordered her sister. "And don't forget to keep a close eye on my costumes while we're in Paris. Remember how they were almost stolen last time?"

Cornélia was not the only member of the diva's coterie when she went on tour.

Albani now employed a secretary and a personal maid. There was also Beauty, the Maltese terrier that followed Emma everywhere and waited for her backstage during her performances. "You're my only pet, now that my nightingale, Philomèle, who echoes my voice, can't sing anymore: he's ill and had to stay home," Emma told the little dog. "But I'm warning you, don't come onstage barking and jump on me, like you did at Covent Garden!"

The press kept Albani's London fans up to date on her Parisian performances. A British correspondent wrote:

"Miss Albani's success at the Théâtre Italien in Paris grows with every performance. It is a great pity that French fanaticism prevents the presentation of *Lohengrin* here: Albani's sweet rendering of Elsa would reconcile the Parisians to Wagner."

When she was not performing, the young diva was invited to various society receptions. She met members of the great aristocratic families of France, as well as eminent republican personalities. She was received at the Élysée Palace, where she sang before the President and his guests. She wrote to her father: "The Marshall of France, Patrice de MacMahon, Duke of Magenta and President of the French Republic, received me at his official residence, for a recital. He and his wife paid me very generously and presented me with a lovely little Sèvres porcelain sculpture group[1] from the last century. I was extremely flattered and deeply honoured."

Like many notables of the day, Albani decided that it was fitting to have her portrait painted.

"By whom?" asked her sister.

"Will Hicock Low. Don't you remember him?"

Low, who hailed from Albany, was currently living in Paris.[2] Emma arrived at his studio accompanied by Mary, her maid, who lugged carpetbags stuffed with opera costumes. Emma tried the costumes on, and they discussed the merits of each for the purposes of Albani's portrait.

The prima donna and the painter finally chose the costume from *Lucia di Lammermoor*, for its pleasing combination of aquamarine, burgundy, and white. With

---

1. Now in the collection of the Société d'histoire de la Seigneurie de Chambly.
2. Low (1853-1932) studied under Gérôme from 1873 to 1877. He is known for his stained glass work and mural panels.

it, Emma wore the pearl cross and necklace that Queen Victoria had given her two years before. The background of the painting would be plain, to make the subject stand out better.

The artist perfectly captured the steely determination in Albani's eyes, the slightly childish pout of her mouth, and her luxuriant dark curly hair.[1]

Years later, giving an account of the numerous sittings that had been necessary for the portrait, Emma said: "It was so draughty in that studio that I caught a terrible cold. Fortunately, it was during a two-week holiday from my schedule!"

In June 1877, Emma sang the role of Senta in *Die fliegende Holländer* (known in English as *The Flying Dutchman*). She was fascinated by the poetic aspect of Wagnerian opera: its otherworldly atmosphere inundated by light and colours; its fantastically costumed heroines in enchanted, epic settings. Wagner's celestial harmonies transported the audience into a phantasmagorical world that echoed the taste of the times for spiritism. Rapid technological advances in the nineteenth century had allowed possibilities never dreamed of before. Stage designers were now able to create sets and effects of imaginative splendour, bringing onto the stage real ships, live horses, railway cars, hot-air balloons, cannons and smoke, rain, snow, waterfalls, stormy seas, lightning bolts, fires, and even earthquakes. It happened occasionally that, when faced with such realistic catastrophes, opera-goers would panic and flee the theatre!

1. The portrait is now part of the collection of the Musée du Québec.

International Star

At the Handel Festival held in London's Crystal Palace, Albani was engaged to sing a main role in a majestic work: the *Messiah*. Twenty-one thousand people crowded into the gigantic glass structure to attend performances by four thousand choral singers and musicians. Considering the monumental size of the Palace and the number of people in the choir and orchestra, Emma wondered if her voice would carry sufficiently. However, her fears were allayed during rehearsals. Emma remembered what Clara Novello, the great oratorio singer, had said: "Oratorio supplies no fictitious aids of scenery, impersonation, or story to bring the audience into sympathy with the singer. It is just music in its purest, boldest form."

Emma returned in triumph to Paris to perform *La traviata*. "Violetta is a superb role, but a dangerous one," she confided to a French newspaper reporter. "The aria of the first act ends in a high half-tone. If a singer doesn't carry it off, nothing can save the rest of the performance: the audience will lose interest."

She did carry it off. Albani's Violetta was praised to the skies. This particular character, dear to French hearts, is modelled after Marguerite Gauthier, the heroine of the novel, *La Dame aux camélias*, by Alexandre Dumas Fils. All French-speaking actresses dream of being able to play Marguerite one day.

Albani was at the height of her glory. Still in Paris, she created *Alma Incantatrice*, written for her by Friedrich von Flotow, the composer of *Martha*. She also sang in *Rigoletto* and several other operas. One evening, a group of art students in the audience executed a set of sketches of Emma performing, and presented them to her as a tribute. One of the drawings was signed Sargent.[1]

An anecdote was doing the rounds of the Parisian cafés and salons:

A young dandy called his friend on that new invention, the telephone – a machine with bells and a crank, which transmitted nasal tones on a line that frequently went dead. "*Allô, mon cher;* are you going to the Baronne's tonight?" "No, my friend," was the reply. "I have been Albanized: I'm going back to the Théâtre Italien!"

Was the idolization of Albani in Paris glibness, or was it sincere admiration? It was certainly a bit of both. At that moment, however, the object of the adulation did not really care one way or the other, for she was preoccupied by a matter of a completely different nature. On her return to London, she would make a surprise announcement to her public.

---

1. British painter John Singer Sargent.

8

Happiness in London, Fiasco in Milan

Emma was returning to London for a particularly personal reason: her approaching marriage. Her fans were taken completely unawares by the announcement; the letters and cheques the diva received from her numerous admirers had always been promptly sent back, with her father, Joseph Lajeunesse, usually carrying out that duty. Even so, rumours had been circulating that Albani was betrothed to a worldly Italian prince who had occasionally been privileged to escort her out to supper. The English public had been disconcerted by the danger of losing their favourite songstress to a foreigner. On the other hand, in the Victorian era, a woman who had not married before the age of thirty

Albani on vacation in Scotland, with her husband Ernest Gye and their son Ernest Frederick, who was born in 1879.

was viewed as an old maid, and Emma would turn thirty that November.

Although she turned the tables on the gossips by revealing that they had been a long way off base, Albani provided more fodder for speculation by choosing Ernest Gye for her life's companion. She had known Frederick Gye's son since she first arrived in London, and the two had become well acquainted during Emma's tour of the United States. Ernest had taken over from his father as her impresario, and they had naturally grown closer to each other. Ernest had discreetly courted Emma for several months before asking her to marry him one evening as they sat together on a loveseat in the Gyes' drawing room. He punctiliously observed the proper form by asking her father to bless their union.

In the London artistic milieu, tongues wagged. "She's marrying him to advance her career"; "Gye Senior arranged the match to keep his star attraction at Covent Garden"; and "It's pure humbug! Ernest is really in love with Albani's sister – that's why Cornélia was sent off to teach music to the children of the Spanish Royal Family" were among the comments heard.

In spite of these malicious darts, the wedding took place as planned in London on August 6, 1878, at the Catholic Church of the Assumption, an imposing eighteenth-century building. The ceremony itself was simple, with only a few friends, relatives, and fellow singers in attendance.

A larger number of people were invited to Ernest and Emma's wedding reception held outdoors at the

Gyes' country house, under a grand striped pavilion. Guests strolled among rosebushes on emerald-green lawns, and the couple received sumptuous wedding gifts, crystal and silverware vying in elegance.

The newlyweds set up residence at Boltons, a well-appointed house in Kensington, London. Their staff consisted of a secretary, a cook, and a chambermaid. When Cornélia's contract at the Spanish Court ended, she moved in with her sister and her husband and resumed her duties as Albani's accompanist. Nelly also gave piano lessons, receiving her pupils at home. "My sister is perched at the top of the ladder; I must hold it steady down below," she would say.

Joseph Lajeunesse returned to Canada to spend the last years of his life in Chambly, in the comfortable little house that Emma had bought for him. He left England with his daughter's single-row harp; Queen Victoria had given her a magnificent two-row instrument a few years before.

In October, Albani suddenly felt ill after a performance; she barely managed to reach her dressing room before falling onto a sofa in a dead faint. After reviving her sister, Cornélia anxiously told her that she must see a doctor.

"No, Nelly, please, I'm fine – it's just a bit of overwork."

"Could our prima donna be expecting a happy event?" asked the tenor of that evening's programme, with a wink at Cornélia.

The next morning, as well as the following three mornings, Emma felt distinctly nauseated. She consented to be examined by Dr. Bryant of Harley Street, who cheerfully confirmed her suspicions. "Congratulations, Madame Albani. You are expecting a child!"

Emma replied distractedly to the physician's warm good wishes, thinking: *I'm leaving on tour to Moscow soon... I have a tendency to gain weight: will I ever get my figure back after a pregnancy?* She comforted herself by thinking of the faithful Cornélia. *Nelly will take care of it. She loves to knit. We'll have a nanny, of course, but Nelly will be quite happy to manage the baby, as she does the rest of the household.* Emma also pictured the exquisite christening robe that the cloistered Sisters of the Sacred Heart would surely sew and embroider for the baby. A fleeting smile played about her lips, but abruptly, sharp anxiety halted her imaginings. *Maman died in childbirth... the same thing might happen to me!* As Emma and Ernest returned home in their carriage, Ernest was perplexed by his wife's apparent lack of excitement at the prospect.

Backstage, it was whispered that the diva did not want a child, at least not at that moment, when her career was at its height.

Albani left for Russia in November, ignoring warnings that she should curtail her activities. She had never forgotten the Tsar, and her heart beat fast at the thought of seeing him again, even though she was now married and was accompanied by her husband. The *cantatrice* brought crowds to their feet throughout the tour; she possessed the power of winning the spontaneous acclaim of the public, a gift reserved for heads of state and great artists.

In Moscow, she relived the same emotions she had felt on her first visit. She performed in the same theatre, although her repertoire was different; it included *Tannhäuser*, *La traviata*, and *Faust* this time. After her last performance of Faust in St Petersburg, Tsar Alexander sent her a colossal bouquet of flowers.

But on December 4, Ernest received a telegram informing him that his father had met with a serious hunting accident on the estate of his friend, Lord Dillon, in Oxfordshire. Ernest's parting words as he left Emma in the Tsar's capital were "Take care of yourself, my darling. Pray that I may arrive in time!" Unfortunately, Gye Senior was dead before his son reached England.

Distraught, Ernest was obliged to remain in London to see to his father's affairs. Taking up the reins from an exceptionally energetic and enterprising man like Frederick Gye was not an easy task.

Emma returned home at long last. She had several engagements left to fulfil before taking the first rest of her career: she would be away from the opera for a period of several months.

Ernest Frederick Gye was born on June 4, 1879. He was an undemanding infant who seemed to have inherited his father's placid temperament. Albani had controlled herself rigidly during his birth, even refraining from crying out so as not to injure her vocal chords. "I would prefer ten major opera roles over the experience of childbirth," she declared. "I will not endure it a second time!"

News of the happy event reached Covent Garden the next morning, while the orchestra was rehearsing. In homage to the new scion of the Gye family, the conductor interrupted the rehearsal and launched the orchestra into an excerpt from Handel's oratorio, *Judas Maccabaeus*: "Hail, the Conquering Hero!"

Albani was now in full possession of her art. Her career was fulfilling every promise; marriage and motherhood seemed to have brought about a new blossoming in her. Full of confidence, Emma prevailed upon her husband: "Ernest, my sweet, I'd like you to organize a programme in Milan for me. I want to be the first Canadian soprano to sing at La Scala."

The world's most celebrated opera house willingly engaged the Covent Garden sensation for a series of performances in 1880. After all, Albani had won remarkable critical successes in Florence, Nice, and Brussels, where she had sung her Italian opera roles in the original language while the rest of the company sang in French. La Scala audiences, however, were mistrustful of anyone or anything that was not Italian.

Albani's first appearance in Milan was in the difficult title role of *Lucia di Lammermoor*. Before the performance, she felt tired and the management of La Scala had suggested that she was "not in voice," but nothing could convince her not to sing that night. The audience reacted coldly to her valiant effort, and she was hissed and hooted. The tenor, greatly offended, walked off the stage. The diva attempted to impose herself, but it was useless: the hissing and catcalls continued unabated. Emma abandoned the struggle and collapsed in tears backstage, convinced that jealous rivals had paid members of the audience to boo her off the stage.

Deeply mortified, she prepared to leave her beloved Italy. "Darling, it was your first and only fiasco," said her husband, trying to console her. "You'll see: your London fans will set things right again."

Ernest was not mistaken. Albani was warmly applauded at her first Covent Garden appearance of the 1880 season. The *Daily Telegraph* reported: "Miss Albani's return occasioned an enthusiastic welcome. An artist who upholds the dignity of her profession in the eyes of the public, and whose private life is irreproachable, she is appreciated by everyone."

It was true that Emma's career was astonishingly free from scandal. Her conduct was prudish compared to that of some of the other famous singers and actresses of the period – Sarah Bernhardt, for example. La Grande Sarah was still being talked about after her visit to London during a tour of Great Britain with the Comédie Française. She had seduced the Prince of Wales and had let her pet leopard loose among the Prince's terrified servants.

The year after her Milan debacle, Emma's peace of mind was again deeply shaken when she learned that the Tsar had been assassinated in St Petersburg by a Nihilist bomb. "He was a marvellous man, and very humane," said Emma to her sister. "He liberated the serfs in Russia, and was paid for it by being murdered. How unjust!"

Emma's desolate mood was reflected in her behaviour towards her domestic employees. One morning, she lost patience when the chambermaid failed to appear with her breakfast after she had repeatedly rung the electric bell to summon her. "Mary!" chided the mistress of the house when the breakfast tray was finally brought, "Don't these new bells ring loudly enough? One cannot be served properly anymore!"

"Please'm, forgive me," answered Mary, pulling back the curtains to reveal the grey, drizzling morning outside. "I got the trays wrong; I had to go back to the kitchen to get yours, with your black tea. You're singing tonight, and I know milk is so bad for your voice!"

"On top of that," snapped the diva, "I hardly slept at all! These tramways are atrociously noisy!"

Even while deploring the racket of the rattling trams, Emma appreciated many of the benefits of electricity. The Savoy Theatre of London was first theatre to be entirely equipped with electric lighting. Of course, the managers of the Savoy could afford it; their Gilbert and Sullivan productions filled the house – and the coffers – every evening. Emma fervently hoped that Covent Garden Theatre would follow suit, and the sooner the better.

"She's awfully touchy this morning," thought Mary. "And usually, she's so kind. I'd better watch my step today!"

"Tonight," said Emma, "I'm giving a private recital[1] at Lord and Lady Dudley's. You'll prepare my pigeon's-throat-grey dress," she ordered.

The dress was ready for Emma when she went into her chamber to change for her evening engagement. Mary was on hand to dress her mistress's hair and to sponge her face and shoulders with warm water.

1. Private concerts were very popular among the aristocracy; there was great competition to obtain the artists most in vogue for these musical soirées.

Young Mrs. Gye submitted to these ministrations, then left the room, silently but for the swishing of silk.

Later that year, Albani was engaged to sing at a benefit concert in aid of the victims of a recent flood in the Low Countries. The King and Queen of Belgium were going to lend their presence to the event. Cornélia advised Emma: "There won't be any fee, but it will be good for your reputation." Emma did not deign to reply. Decidedly, she was awfully touchy these days!

Albani sang the role of Tamara in Anton Rubinstein's *The Demon*. This opera, created six years before in St. Petersburg, was considered the composer's masterpiece, and he was directing it himself. It was the ideal performance situation; Emma forgot her unhappiness and immersed herself in her work.

Following this success, she sang at her beloved provincial festivals in England, and toured both Scotland and Ireland.

During the tour, Ernest brought her news of a special invitation.

"My darling, the director of the Berlin Royal Opera House has asked you to sing *Lohengrin* there, with the best Wagnerian singers."

"In German, for the Germans! I feel I can carry off a triumph that hasn't been seen for a long time – one that will make everyone forget about Milan!"

Albani recovered all her former high spirits in this formidable German adventure. Berlin was a pompously grandiose and excitingly cosmopolitan city. Although he was not an opera-lover, Emperor Wilhelm I attended several of Emma's performances, and bestowed upon

International Star

her the honorary title of *Hofkammersängerin*, or royal court singer. She would have a more marked success later with Wilhelm's successor, Kaiser Wilhelm II, a true opera connoisseur. However, the aged Empress Augusta did not miss any of Albani's performances; in spite of her fragile health, she would have herself pushed in a wheelchair along a special corridor that linked the palace to the opera house and the imperial box.

The *Berliner Zeitung* wrote: "*Das Albani* interpreted the very difficult and poetic character of Elsa with such consummate mastery that the audience was aroused by her to enthusiasm."

The correspondent of *The Times* wired his byline to London: "Madame Albani appeared tonight as Elsa, singing her part in the native German. The house was crowded to the very ceiling and extravagant prices were paid for seats. Madame Albani achieved what may well be called a complete triumph, greater even than any she has won hitherto."

Berlin high society showered the diva and her husband with invitations. The couple was asked to dine at the residence of the Austrian ambassador. At table, Emma found herself beside a man who was attached to the household of the Crown Princess Frederika. He told her: "Her Highness knew I would see you tonight. She asked me to give you this." He handed Emma a telegram that Queen Victoria had cabled to her cousin a few days before. It read: "Am anxious to recommend Madame Albani to you. She is my Canadian subject, an excellent person, known to me, a splendid artiste and I take much interest in her. The Queen."

The following day, the Crown Princess received Albani and her husband at home. She possessed a phonograph, recently invented, and showed them how it worked. She had a record of the diva performing, and thus, Albani heard herself singing for posterity for the first time. In spite of the distortion of the earliest recordings, this machine soon became all the rage and fascinated everyone who heard it.

Emma was given the opportunity to sing Gounod's oratorio, *Rédemption*, at the Birmingham Festival of 1882, under the composer's direction. Gounod liked the Canadian soprano's voice so much that he promised to compose a new work for her to create.

Not long into the new year, Emma learned that Richard Wagner, whose health had rapidly declined, was dying in Venice. She was affected by the sad news. "It is a terrible loss for modern music. If I had more time, we would take the train to Venice to contemplate the places he loved and wanted to see before bidding farewell to the world." Daydreaming, she imagined herself in the dining car of the elegant Orient Express train with its mahogany panelling and crystal chandeliers, its waiters dressed in black and white transporting bottles of champagne to tables covered in snowy linen and topped by vases of fresh-cut flowers.

Ernest brought his wife gently back to reality: "It would be better to prepare for your tour of the United States and Canada, my darling."

Emma harboured a lingering bitterness towards her homeland. "My fellow *Canadiens* want to make it up to me," she thought. "It's easy for them, now that

I'm well-known all over the world: they don't have to take a chance on me."

Wagner breathed his last while Albani and her husband, as well as fellow opera star Adelina Patti, her impresario, and their small troupe, were aboard the *Pavonia*, sailing from Liverpool to New York.[1] The two-week crossing was a bad one, and Emma spent all but two days of it in her bunk, prostrated by seasickness. She arrived in New York greatly weakened and late for her rehearsals. In spite of this, she was ready on time for the scheduled performances.

After her twenty-year absence, Emma was eagerly awaited in Montreal. She was welcomed as an official guest: a reception committee met her at the American border and brought her into the city on a private railway car. A crowd of ten thousand greeted her as the train drew into Bonaventure Station. The snow-covered streets appeared fairy-like; members of the Snowshoe Club, dressed in their sporting outfits and carrying flaming torches, lined each side of the street when Albani and company emerged from the building.

Emma whispered happily to Ernest: "Snowshoeing was my favourite sport when I was a girl." A brass band struck up the traditional *"Vive la Canadienne"* as Emma and her friends climbed into the two sleighs assigned to take them to the Windsor Hotel. Having performed in Boston the previous evening, Emma was exhausted, but how could she have resisted such a fervent salute? She forgot her aching head and smiled at the cheering crowds.

1. "Concert parties" were popular in these days: opera singers would go on tour with other singers and musicians.

Emma's father was waiting at the hotel. After happy greetings on all sides, he told her that tickets for her concerts at Queen's Hall on March 27, 29, and 31 varied in price from three to five dollars, and that special trains had been scheduled for those evenings to bring people into the city from outlying areas.

A reception in Albani's honour was organized the next day at Montreal's city hall. Emma was seated on the mayor's throne. After the official speeches, Ernest spoke to express thanks on his wife's behalf. "Tell them how happy they've made me," she whispered as he rose to his feet. The ceremony ended with the reading of an ode written for Emma by Louis-Honoré Fréchette, Quebec's most recognized poet. Her eyes blurred with tears as she listened to the last verse:

> 'Tis no matter; with the confession of our expiated sins,
> Allow us to lay at your feet, Albani,
> All our best wishes, which, tonight, merge as one!
> Yonder, you were given fame and fortune;
> Your country, proud of you, comes to offer in its turn
> Its most fervent tribute and its most tender love.

Emma remained on the dais for over two hours afterwards, shaking hands with hundreds of admirers. Montreal's stores and offices were closed that day, and the streets thronged with people celebrating her return home.

∞

At her recitals, when Emma sang *Souvenirs d'un jeune âge*, an aria from the opera *La Pré aux clercs* by Ferdinand Hérold that ends with the words: "*Rendez-moi ma patrie, ou laissez-moi mourir,*"[1] the audience would stand and applaud lustily, sometimes for more than five minutes. The score of this aria was republished, with Albani's photograph on the cover page, and it came to be considered a Québécois national song.

One journalist wrote: "Last night at Queen's Hall, the public was beside itself. There wasn't a seat left in the balcony, where several people remained standing for the entire performance. Madame Albani possesses a voice of exquisite tenderness."

To show her appreciation for the way she had been welcomed in Montreal, the international star who had been "the little Lajeunesse girl" donated five hundred dollars from her concert takings to the mayor's office, to be distributed among the city's poor.

Fortunately, Emma had enough free time to see old friends and relatives. She visited her father, her brother Adélard, who was now a priest, and even her grandmother Rachel in the begonia-surrounded house in Chambly. And the great Emma Albani proudly went to sing *Ave Maria* in the chapel of the Sacred Heart Convent in Sault-au-Recollet, where she had sung so joyfully as a young *pensionnaire* many years before.

Naturally, Emma was moved by all this attention and heartfelt gestures of appreciation. However, for her, "home, sweet home" was now England.

---

1. "Give me back my country or let me die."

Albani during one of her numerous Atlantic crossings, with her husband Ernest and (probably) her sister Cornélia.

9

The Star Fades

"Roberto, blacken the sides of my gown, please," Albani told the costume assistant at Covent Garden. It was the dress rehearsal of Gounod's *Roméo et Juliette*, in which Emma was singing the role of the tragic heroine.

"But, Madame, it has already been done."

"Do it again, then. And don't roll your eyes at me! I'm not the only one making demands here. You've already heightened the tenor's heels so that his voice will project more; you've loosened his shirt so he can breathe better, and you've changed his velvet jacket for a brocade one that won't absorb the sound as much!"

"She's only taking her stage jitters out on me," said the costume assistant to himself. "I should be used to it by now!"

Albani was thirty-six years old that season, while Juliette, the heroine of the play and the opera, is supposed to be fifteen. The great *cantatrice* was still able to create the necessary illusion on stage to fit her roles – resorting to the occasional artifice, such as darkening the sides of her costumes to appear slimmer. In any case, opera-lovers are notably blind to physical shortcomings as long as the singer's voice is worth listening to, and Albani's voice was still in full flower.

In spite of her continuing worldwide success, it seemed that people were beginning to lack the appropriate reverence towards the diva – perhaps because Ernest Gye was no longer in charge of Covent Garden. The theatre had declined under his directorship, and he had resigned as its manager. The official reason given out was that Ernest had decided to dedicate all his energies to managing his wife's career.

This did not prevent Albani from triumphing in *Lohengrin* – sung in German – at the same Covent Garden Theatre. Emma was able to savour her victory more sweetly after the opera and the festival season ended, ensconced in a country residence that one of her admirers, Lord Fife, had offered for her use the previous year.

Old Mar Lodge was a large hunting pavilion in the valley of the River Dee in the Scottish Highlands, in a landscape of lakes, islands, forests, and hills that reminded Emma of Canada. However, the mysterious countryside, along with its relics of battles among the clans and the piercing notes of the bagpipes, was pure Scottish. Albani and her family would sojourn for vacations in the land of Donizetti's Lucia and Verdi's Lady Macbeth for five years.[1]

The estate was only a few miles away from Balmoral, the castle belonging to the Queen. Victoria was the first neighbour to extend a friendly invitation to the Gyes.

As time went on, it became customary for Emma to sing, accompanying herself on the piano, at intimate receptions at Balmoral. Victoria, lulled by the music and the warmth from the open hearth, would often drift into slumber. Once, she was rudely awakened when Emma fell onto the carpet at her feet; a leg of the piano bench had suddenly given way. The Queen, still half asleep, unthinkingly uttered her famous stock phrase, the severe "We are not amused," and the guests burst into laughter at the incongruity of the situation.

Emma returned Victoria's invitation, and the Queen came to the Lodge for tea on several occasions. The young Ernest Frederick was impressed: "Oh, Mummy, what a little woman for such a big queen!" he said one day.

These holidays in Scotland were the only times that the boy could see both his parents as much as he liked. What joy! His father took him on expeditions into the hills, and his mother read him *Peter Rabbit* and other Beatrix Potter stories before he went to bed. Knowing that she would go off on a singing engagement all too soon, he would hug her tightly.

1. In her autobiography, Emma recalled these stays at Old Mar Lodge with fondness.

When the holidays ended, Emma would return to London, and the season of opera performances and festival recitals would start up again. In 1885, she sang again in the Handel Festival at the Crystal Palace,[1] and at the Birmingham Festival, where she created a new oratorio, *Mors et Vita*, composed for her by Charles Gounod.[2] The composer and the soprano collaborated together in preparing the concert; he addressed her as "my dear great interpreter," and rewrote certain sections of the score that Emma found difficult.

Queen Victoria attended the first performance of the oratorio and invited Albani back to Balmoral; Emma had become a regular member of the royal entourage in Scotland. Victoria took out a page of her diary and gave it to Emma, after writing on it: "To Madame Albani-Gye, with my warmest thanks for the great pleasure I had upon hearing her sing. – Victoria Regina, Balmoral Castle, September 24, 1885." Emma kept it carefully among her most valued souvenirs, among tributes from Gounod, Brahms, and Franz Liszt.

Liszt came to London in April 1886 for the premiere performance of his oratorio, *The Legend of St. Elizabeth*, created by Albani. Emma was in awe of the illustrious black-caped composer with the face of an ascetic – by this time, he had been ordained a Franciscan and styled himself the Abbé Liszt. After the performance, he wrote to thank Emma and expressed

---

1. Albani starred in the Handel Festival at the Crystal Palace every year for two decades.
2. Other composers who wrote music for Albani included Antonín Dvořák and Arthur Sullivan, who became one of her greatest friends.

his admiration for her art. She never saw Liszt again: he died later that year.

Albani had a gift for inspiring composers. A few years later, during a tour of Austria, Hungary, and Bohemia, she met Johannes Brahms in Vienna. He reportedly wept when he heard her sing his *Requiem*.

At the beginning of the 1887 Berlin opera season, Albani sang Lohengrin and *Die fliegande Holländer* in German, and *La traviata*, *Rigoletto*, and *Faust* in Italian.

Her valise bulging with musical scores, Emma crisscrossed Europe, returning to Covent Garden to sing Antonida in *A Life for the Tsar* by Mikhail Glinka – the story of a peasant hero who died saving the first Romanoff tsar in 1613. The work brought back poignant memories of St. Petersburg, where Albani's fresh beauty and innocence had captured Russian hearts. Now, she was almost forty and would soon begin an inevitable decline as far as her singing voice was concerned.

But Albani hadn't yet reached that precarious stage, and Ernest arranged her third North American tour. In January 1889, they set sail for Canada on the *Etruria*, accompanied by a convivial party of other talented singers and musicians. Rehearsals were held every day of the voyage; on rough days, the piano had to be bolted to the floor.

The steamer made its entry into the scenic Gulf of St. Lawrence. When Albani and her troupe disembarked at Quebec City, they lodged at the Château Frontenac Hotel, with its sweeping view of the river. Emma was invited to the Quebec provincial parliament and was the guest of honour at the luncheon given by Premier Honoré Mercier after the morning's session.

"The weather here is pleasant; I hope it will still be so at the time of your visit," wrote Sir John A. Macdonald, enjoining Emma and her husband to stay at Earnscliffe, the prime minister's official residence perched on a cliff overlooking the Ottawa River. The couple travelled to the national capital in a private railway car provided by William Van Horne, the president of the Canadian Pacific Railway; it was lavishly fitted with beds, a parlour, and a kitchen.

They enjoyed their time in the nation's raw new capital; Ernest even went tobogganing with Sir John!

After a zigzag into the United States, their itinerary took them to Montreal, where Albani gave the farewell concert of her tour. This city also had its *château*: a huge castle built entirely of ice! A masterpiece of the imagination, with towers and turrets hacked from the frozen St. Lawrence River, and illuminated by electric lights, it gleamed and sparkled in the night.

In the sleigh that carried her to the performance hall, the diva hummed some of the arias and songs she would perform that evening. She glanced fondly at the familiar passing scene: the snow-filled streets, passers-by hailing horse-drawn taxis, and children hurling snowballs that burst against greystone buildings that reminded her of parts of The City, London's business district.

Emma arrived back in London for the start of the opera season. She sang for the Shah of Persia during his official visit to England in July 1889. The potentate was resplendent in his uniform, glittering with diamonds and other precious stones – he shone more brilliantly than a jewellery shop window. The Shah, amused by the sight of the musicians tuning their instruments, applauded; for etiquette's sake, the rest of the audience imitated him. He slept through most of the performance, rousing himself every once in a while to admire the ballerinas. When he wondered aloud if he might obtain some of them for his harem, he was told that in England, these arrangements were made more discreetly.

It was during that season that Nelly Melba made her Covent Garden debut in *Rigoletto*. The wide range and beautiful timbre of her voice, the quality of her phrasing, and her exceptional lung capacity immediately made her the house darling.

Emma realized that Albani's star was fading at last. In the newspapers she read that "the Covent Garden management has decided to stop basing its opera programme on the cult of a single star performer. Now, secondary roles as well will be sung by great artists. Nonetheless, we deplore the loss of Madame Albani, who has enchanted audiences of the Royal Italian Opera in her grand roles for many a year. In future, she will no longer have the exclusivity of these roles."

George Bernard Shaw, the sharp-tongued Irish playwright, essayist, and man-about-town, was a relentless critic of Albani and other opera divas. He wrote of Emma: "her acting is calculated, with an obvious lack of spontaneity." He admitted, however, that she was unsurpassed as an interpreter of Wagner's music.

Emma was still in demand for touring contracts, and her busy schedule did not allow her to ruminate on comments such as Shaw's. In autumn 1889, she left for a tour of the United States and Mexico as part of a troupe that included the legendary Adelina Patti and Francesco Tamagno. On its way to Mexico City, the large convoy of opera stars, musicians, and choral singers, with their mountains of baggage containing costumes, instruments, and stage sets, were obliged to delay for a day until a stretch of the railway track could be repaired, completely throwing them off their tour schedule.

Mexico City is situated at an altitude of over two thousand metres; the nights are chilly, and most of the houses and hotels are unheated. Emma warmed herself by drinking the fortifying cordial that she had used for years, a concoction called Mariani wine. Charles Gounod had introduced her to the benefits of this elixir based on pulverized coca leaves. Newspaper advertisements of the period proclaimed that "Mariani wine stimulates and clears the throat and strengthens the chest. Approved by the Medical Academy of Paris, this drink has gone around the world. It is known as 'the wine of athletes.'"

From Mexico, the troupe returned to the United States, then to Canada, where Emma sang *La traviata* and *Lucia di Lammermoor*. It was the first time in Canada that two full-length operas were presented by a troupe mounted for the occasion. Albani's visit ended in Montreal with a benefit concert in aid of the Notre-Dame Hospital. Held at the Victoria skating rink, this event brought in twenty-five hundred dollars.

The following year, at Covent Garden, she sang Desdemona in Verdi's *Otello*, opposite Jean de Reszke, who sang the role of the jealous Moor. In Albani's dressing room hung a photograph of the celebrated tenor, inscribed: "With the very affectionate homage of her devoted partner."

True to himself, George Bernard Shaw wrote of the performance that Desdemona was "pleasantly plump – rather too plump for the role." This barb finally succeeded in annoying Emma. "Him again! Won't he ever leave me in peace?"

To the devil with Shaw! It was no pasty, evanescent Desdemona who gave throat to her first aria, *Mio superbo guerrier*, addressed to Otello, but a passionate and loving wife who poignantly begged for mercy, crying *"Non uccidermi!"*[1] And afterwards, brokenhearted and without hope, intoning *"Emilia, distendi sul mio letto la mia candida veste nuziale se morir dovessi"*[2] before uttering the desperate plea, *"È perchè t'amo che m'uccidi?"*[3] as Otello glares at her with maddened eyes before strangling her.

"De Reszke has the habit of changing the stage directions to maximize the effect, without telling his partners in advance," mused Emma. "I hardly know what to expect: tonight, he's so convincing that I don't know if I'll come out of it alive!" However, after grasping Desdemona's corpse in his arms for the finale, Otello raised her up and led her forward to bow to the wildly applauding crowd.

Glowing with success, she returned to the United States for a three-month contract at the Metropolitan

1. "Don't kill me!"
2. "Emilia, lay my white wedding dress out on my bed, if I must die."
3. "Is it because I love you that you will kill me?"

Opera of New York City. Her Met debut was as Gilda in *Rigoletto* on December 23, 1891.

While Emma and Ernest took the train to Montreal to spend Christmas at the Villa Albani with Papa Lajeunesse, their son Ernest Frederick spent his holidays in England with Aunt Nelly and his paternal relatives. In Chambly, on the Rue Bourgogne, a typically English Christmas dinner was served: turkey, mince pie, and plum pudding. Real candles on the Christmas tree had been replaced by little electric lights. Emma reminded the assembled family members that the tradition of the Christmas tree had been introduced to England by Victoria's beloved Prince Albert, who had brought it from his native Germany.

In Montreal that winter, Albani sang in two operas, with singers from New York. Returning to the Metropolitan, she was acclaimed until the end of March, 1892, in *Faust, Otello, Don Giovanni* (as Elvira), Meyerbeer's *Les Huguenots* (in the role of Valentine), and Wagner's *Lohengrin, Die fliegende Holländer*, and *Die Meistersinger* von Nürnberg (as Eva).

In New York, Albani's name not only appeared in print for her performances, but also her wardrobe: the Redfern shirtwaist dresses that she wore were considered daring. She was also known for wearing hats with fine veils of different hues. "They give rainbow nuances to the face," gushed a feature writer in an American fashion magazine.

In 1893, her career was still in full swing with a demanding agenda of opera tours in Austria, Hungary, and Bohemia, as well as a full slate of English festival performances. A whirlwind schedule, as usual.

International Star

In 1894, Ernest organized for Emma a German tour, which ended in Switzerland where their son was at boarding school. He was fifteen years old and hoped to make a career for himself in the British foreign service. "You'll have to study very hard, Freddy," his father advised him. "You know how difficult the civil service entrance exams are."

In the train on their way back to England, Emma said to her husband: "How Freddy has grown! I hardly know him, really, being so busy with my singing and all the travelling. When he was little, we used to take him with us, but those days ended so soon. Do you remember how he used to hang on to us, begging us not to go? And when he was ten, how he learned my part in *Mors et Vita* by heart so we would return more quickly to hear him sing it? And the drawings of us he used to do when we were away? I don't believe he has ever really understood how much I love him, in spite of everything."

Two years later, Albani was booked for a new North American concert tour at the beginning of 1896. New York City seemed more electrifying than ever; the first public cinema screenings had just been inaugurated and were attracting eager crowds.

On this trip, Ernest Frederick accompanied his parents. He was now a handsome youth of seventeen, but very reserved, having been brought up under the Victorian edict that children were to be seen and not heard. He was all eyes and ears on the tour, as he took in new impressions. When they reached Quebec City, it was Carnival time, with its opening ceremonies of military parades. His mother sang, accompanied by two hundred choristers, a violinist, and the combined bands of the Royal Canadian Artillery, the Quebec Rifles, and the Canadian Hussars. Before sailing for England, the Gyes visited Chambly, where Ernest Frederick saw his maternal grandfather for the first time in many years. "It's a beautiful country," he told the aging Joseph Lajeunesse. "I'll come back for a holiday as soon as I can."

The return to London was tinged with sorrow, as it was to be Albani's last season at Covent Garden. Her final repertoire there was a celebration of the three great opera composers, Mozart, Meyerbeer, and Wagner. The critics all agreed that Albani's rendering of the *Liebestod,* Isolde's great love song to the dead Tristan, was the apogee of her art. Over the years, Emma's voice had gained in substance and had deepened from the lighter coloratura soprano to the dramatic soprano style suitable for the role of Isolde.

Thus, Albani left the stage where she had shone so brightly for twenty-four years of her career and gracefully made way for the younger soprano stars. Nonetheless, it was painful for her to strip her dressing room of all the lovingly placed evidence of her long reign at Covent Garden: the silver candlesticks, her red brocade divan, her Venetian mirror. This had been her second home.

To raise her spirits, Emma went to take a thermal cure in Auvergne in south-central France. "The waters here are a sovereign elixir for the throat and bronchial tubes," she wrote to her devoted friend, the poet Louis Fréchette. She was to see him soon, for a cross-Canada Albani tour was scheduled for November 1896.

Touring a country of such vast dimensions was not without problems. In Calgary, for example, the lighting was inadequate; for the garden scene in *Faust*, a locomotive headlamp was brought in! Some of the newspaper critics along the way were lukewarm towards Emma's performances. From the *Hamilton Spectator*: "Her voice no longer has the freshness and purity that it once had. There are signs of exhaustion in the high register. The quality is slightly laborious and the intonation hesitant. However, the voice remains full and ample, and is carried with the art and subtlety that have made Miss Albani one of the great artists of our time."

Emma felt a sense of panic when she read these comments. Was the end of her career at hand? One thing she knew for certain: she was getting old.

In 1925, King George V conferred on Albani
the title Dame Commander of the British Empire.

10

The Curtain Falls

1897. Albani was fifty years old, and it was Victoria's Diamond Jubilee, marking the sixtieth year of her reign. "My dear friend," the monarch wrote to Emma, "we are greatly pleased: imagine that we were captured in the first moving pictures during our Jubilee Parade! It is very tiring for the eyes to view it, but such a marvel is certainly worth a headache."

At the Gyes' home in Kensington, money no longer flowed as freely as it had in the past. Although Cornélia had increased the number of her piano pupils, Emma was obliged to go on tour in increasingly far-flung corners of the world to earn enough to keep the family. She did not sign these touring contracts strictly for the income they would bring her; she wanted to feel that the great Albani was still appreciated – even though, by now, odd sounds would occasionally escape her throat.

In 1898, she toured South Africa and Australia for the first time.

The following year, she sang *Lohengrin* in England for the Queen, at Windsor Castle this time. Victoria, with her German background, had always been an avid Wagner fan. At the same time, Albani continued to give recitals while keeping up her career as an oratorio soloist.[1]

The twentieth century ushered in a new generation of opera divas, some of whom flouted Victorian convention. Soprano Lina Cavalieri kissed Enrico Caruso on the lips in Giordano's *Fedora*[2] at the Met in New York, a theatrical touch that had never been seen before. Scottish soprano Mary Garden shocked audiences by her striptease during the "Dance of the Seven Veils" in Richard Strauss's *Salome*; some people said this was to be expected, as she was the soprano who had created that very strange opera, *Pelléas et Mélisande*, by the young French composer, Claude Debussy. It was an era of great innovation in opera, with startling works by Stravinsky, Janáček, and Prokofiev. It was all so very different from Bellini!

Mercifully, Queen Victoria did not live to witness the upheavals wrought by the changing times, and

1. Versatile singers who performed opera roles, gave recitals, and sang oratorio works were exceptional.
2. Umberto Giordano (1867-1948) also composed the opera *Andrea Chénier*, set during the French Revolution.

International Star

which resulted in the demise of most of the European monarchies. On January 23, 1901, newspaper headlines throughout the world starkly announced "The Queen Is Dead." Victoria died at age eighty-two, after the longest and most glorious reign in the history of the British Empire.

Victoria's eldest son, now King Edward VII, requested that Emma Albani sing at the funeral ceremony, in compliance with his mother's express wishes.

The Queen lay in state at Windsor Castle. The catafalque was covered by the white roses that encircle the English crown. The Royal Family stood in vigil around it: the new King, his wife – now Queen Alexandra – and Victoria and Albert's other children and their families.

A petite woman dressed in black silk, a heavy mourning veil over her face, walked slowly forward as the organ played softly. She stopped before the casket. Her sweet, tender, and very sad voice lifted in song, rendering excerpts from Handel's *Messiah*, the hymns *I Know that My Redeemer Liveth* and *Come unto Him*. It was Albani's first posthumous tribute to her friend and her queen. Louis Fréchette composed a sonnet evoking that moment, entitled *Albani before Queen Victoria's Coffin*. Its final line reads: "Royalty, death, and genius blended their thrice-blessed majesty before God."

Edward, his eyes filled with tears, thanked Albani for her beautiful farewell to his mother. The following year, he invited her to sing at his coronation; on that occasion, Queen Alexandra gave Emma a photograph of herself with a dedication, a much-treasured keepsake.

Emma Albani

After Victoria's death, Emma felt bereft, in spite of the presence of her husband, her sister, and her son, who, although he now lived apart from his parents, had come home to be with his mother for the funeral. Albani had lost a protector and a loyal friend. She looked at the photographs that the monarch had given her. The first was of her coronation, the second of the jubilee, and the third, in a small silver and enamel case, was a miniature portrait of Victoria that Emma took with her everywhere. When she gave it to her, the Queen had said: "I hear that you always carry my photograph with you in your travels. This one will be more convenient for you." Emma strove to shake off her melancholy, and taking her courage in both hands, she resumed her demanding schedule of singing engagements.

Thus, in the months of January and February, 1903, Albani returned to perform in Montreal. The critics were becoming less and less enthusiastic about her. The music critic of *La Presse* wrote: "Albani seems rather tired. Her voice no longer possesses that crystalline purity and that irreproachable *justesse* that constituted its principal charm."

One consolation of the tour was that Emma was able to visit her father. Joseph Lajeunesse died in Chambly the following year at age eighty-three; his son, Adélard, Curé of St. Monique des Deux Montagnes, officiated at the funeral. Shortly afterwards, Emma learned that Ernest Frederick's hopes had been realized: he had been hired by the British Foreign Office.

Inveterate performer that she was, Emma recorded arias and songs for the phonograph, and set

International Star

off on a tour of South Africa. Later, she would tour Australia, New Zealand, India, and Ceylon. Now in her late fifties, she was beginning to be exhausted by her frequent voyages.

Albani made her farewell tour of Canada in 1906. Cornélia, realizing that it might be the last time she would see her country, came along with her sister. Emma sang in Toronto, Ottawa, Sherbrooke, and Sorel. In Montreal, she sang in the Salle Ludger Duvernay of the Monument national[1] and at the Mount Royal Arena. She appeared there with Éva Gauthier, a young Ottawa-born mezzo-soprano and a protégée of Sir Wilfrid Laurier. Instrumentalists and choral singers completed the touring company.

Emma travelled by paddlewheeler from Montreal to Chambly, where she sang for the farmers and their families returning from market. It was an emotional moment, against the backdrop of the setting sun and the calm waters of the Richelieu River. In her home town, every visit by Emma Albani was an occasion for festivities, and every day she spent there comprised a veritable ritual. The diva would wake up at one o'clock in the afternoon and have breakfast in bed. At three o'clock, she would rise and don a satin and lace peignoir to receive her intimate friends. Towards the end of the afternoon, she would leave the house. Very elegantly dressed, with the lower half of her face covered by a black scarf to protect her throat, she would walk along the banks of the river.

1. Albani's photograph still graces the lobby of Salle Ludger Duvernay, and a recent sculpture of her can be seen in the Monument national's Salle des Bronzes.

Emma Albani

In Ottawa, Governor General Earl Grey and Prime Minister Sir Wilfrid Laurier attended an Albani recital. Emma and Ernest were invited several times to the prime minister's residence.

One evening, as they returned to their hotel room, Emma asked her husband: "Don't you find it odd that in a conquered country, a French Canadian is prime minister and rallies the two peoples together?"

"My darling, this harmony is obviously due to the complete freedom given to the French by their English brothers, so that all live together as one large and happy family," was Ernest's complacent reply.

"Nelly would say that the French Canadians have the large families and the English have all the power. Don't you think that's the case?"

"I think it's time you went to bed, my dear!"

The canopied bed was inviting, and the discussion ended there.

Ernest spent his days taking photographs with his Brownie camera. He was like a delighted little boy playing with a new toy. No more cumbersome glass plates, heavy camera body, and unwieldy tripod: the Kodak film was light and practical.

Emma found it much more difficult to leave her homeland this time; she felt as if she were leaving part of her heart there.

Back in London, Albani resumed her usual round of singing engagements, letter-writing, fittings at the dressmaker's, dinner out followed by the opera or the theatre. One such evening in 1906 was memorable: it was Adelina's Patti's farewell recital, after fifty-six years as a performer.

In a letter from the Canadian landscape painter Maurice Cullen, Emma learned that the Ouimetoscope, the first moving picture theatre in North America, had been inaugurated on January 1, 1906. "Sometimes, I leave my studio in the Rue Richelieu in Chambly to treat myself to an evening at the cinema in Montreal," he wrote.

The years were passing quickly, and the soprano's voice showed signs of increasing deterioration. On October 14, 1911, Albani regretfully retired from an active career. Her farewell performance took place at the Albert Hall in London, to a full house that included Sir Arthur Sullivan, Matilde Marchesi, Adelina Patti, Nellie Melba, Emma Calvé, and numerous other notables of the opera world. Emotions ran high; thousands of Albani's fans wept as they listened to her sing Tosti's aria, *Goodbye*. When Emma finally left the stage after repeated ovations by her well-wishers, Cornélia was there to wipe her brow with her handkerchief; Ernest kissed her, and Ernest Frederick embraced his mother, who was trembling like a leaf. The next day's newspapers gave the event the respect Albani was due, reiterating the general opinion that "Madame Albani remains one of the most brilliant musical figures of the nineteenth century."

Emma's nostalgic sadness that year was augmented by the unveiling of Victoria's great funeral monument. In his invitation to her to attend the ceremony, the King reminded Emma, "Her Majesty enjoyed your company very much, and loved your beautiful voice."

Although the occasional newspaper article would mention that the retired opera star "was living quietly in her house in Kensington, giving the odd public recital for the aid of charity," the hidden reality was more difficult. The bare fact was that money was short in the Gye household. Emma acted to replenish the coffers by writing her memoirs in collaboration with a young journalist, Harold Simpson. *Forty Years of Song*, published in London and Toronto in 1911, relates the singer's struggle for perfection and recognition, her rise to prominence, and her glory days at the top of her profession, combined with sketches of many of the great singers, conductors, and composers she had known during her career. Although it is invaluable as a personal chronicle of Albani's life, it reveals a failing memory; inaccuracies in dates and places mar the total effect.

In spite of all she had forgotten, given up, or lost, Emma Albani always retained an unshakable dignity and an imperious manner. Oblivious to the radical changes in fashion that were taking place, particularly during the "Roaring Twenties," she always received her singing students in full-length gowns, festooned in the jewels Queen Victoria had given her. It was difficult to perceive that she was suffering from a lack of ready cash.

In May 1914, the aging *cantatrice* sang Elvira in a private performance of Bellini's *I puritani*. The stage direction of the opera was adapted so that the leading lady would not have to move around the stage very much. Albani now suffered from gallstones and walked with a cane. Nevertheless, she was capable of evoking pathos in Elvira's mad scene.

None of her hardships prevented Albani from receiving guests for five o'clock tea every Saturday afternoon, a custom carried over from her more opulent days. She would pour, wearing an old-fashioned tea gown and displaying her diamonds and her numerous decorations: the Gold Medal of the London Philharmonic Society, the medal of the Belgian Musicians' Association, the Orders of Merit of Denmark and of Saxe-Coburg, Victoria's Jubilee Medal, a decoration from Kaiser Wilhelm I of Germany, and yet another bestowed upon her by the King of the Hawaiian Islands. Emma would show her guests her collection of personal mementoes and would tell them the stories of how she came by the large South American uncut diamond and her other precious gems, her marble bust of a German prince, and a tapestry brought from a faraway land. It was said by some of her visitors that Albani had adopted the regal mannerisms of her dead friend, Victoria.

But the Great War was raging in Europe and things could no longer slide along in their pleasant way. Like many other people, Ernest had been tempted to speculate, and his investments had evaporated. For her part, Emma was ignorant of financial matters, having long ago left this aspect of her life to her husband. She had always been generous to a fault as well as a bit of a spendthrift and did not hesitate to indulge herself as far as money was concerned.

Ernest, no longer able to afford to pay the dues at his club, spent more and more time in pubs. His sister-in-law, Cornélia, defended him: "He has the right to amuse himself a little; it's so dull at home. Ernest Frederick hardly ever comes to see us anymore, and I don't blame him!"

The British Government gave Emma Albani an apartment and granted her an annual pension of one hundred pounds a year because of what they discreetly called "her straitened circumstances." This modest amount did not meet Emma's needs, and she waited hopefully to be called upon to sing in oratorios or to be offered even a minor opera role.

Her voice reduced to a pale imitation of the nightingale's timbre of her youth, she resorted to singing in London music halls and cabarets, in the interludes between variety acts. The audience was made up of working class families, grandparents and parents bouncing the youngsters on their knees. Emma could hardly be heard over the din, and no one paid much attention to her in any case. She executed her pieces conscientiously, but she felt like weeping every time.

The great diva who had been paid the equivalent of twenty thousand Canadian dollars to sing a mass by Rossini in Europe for three months was forced to put her opera costumes up for sale. The second-hand clothing dealers advised Emma to approach a museum or a costume rental establishment.

Soon, Emma gave in to the necessity of selling her jewels, medals, and decorations, which were as much cherished souvenirs of her fame as objects of monetary worth – all for considerably less than their proper value.

The days wore on, each one more disheartening than the one before. Emma would put on the last remaining stage costume that fit her (she had gained a lot of weight) and would faithfully practise her vocalises, awaiting singing contracts that never materialized. She also spent hours listening to her recordings.

Albani's hopes were raised in 1925 when the Canadian prime minister, William Lyon McKenzie King, heard of her distress and proposed that Canada pay her a substantial pension. However, neither the members of the government, nor Alexandre Taschereau, premier of Quebec, went along with the idea. "My country has forgotten me," lamented Emma to her husband, after she had read King's apologetic letter. "But I have never forgotten it: I may have married an Englishman and spent my life in England, but I am still French Canadian at heart."

As a last resort, the Montreal daily *La Presse* organized a public subscription to raise money for the distressed singing legend. The Montreal impresario Louis Bourdon held a charity concert in aid of Albani at the Théâtre St. Denis. He recruited the best musicians, singers, and choristers in the city. CKAC, a local French-language radio station, broadcast the concert live – with a simultaneous transmission to London so that Madame Albani could hear it too. Another recital in the same vein was organized at the Fort de Chambly. The money brought in from these two events totalled about four thousand dollars.

London followed suit at the sympathetic instigation of renowned soprano Nelly Melba. Three days earlier, on May 25, another benefit for Albani had been given under the patronage of Queen Victoria's grandson, His Majesty, George V. Sarah Fischer, a young Canadian soprano who had once studied with Albani and who was enjoying a successful European career, sang at that event.

The money collected in this manner allowed Emma to live out her last years in relative comfort, if not in the style she had once been accustomed to.

Soon after this, the King conferred the Order of Dame of the British Empire upon Emma Lajeunesse Albani Gye, together with an annual pension of three hundred pounds. At the investiture ceremony, Nelly Melba presented Emma with a gigantic bouquet in the shape of a harp. It was a balm for her wounded self-esteem – for a while.

In November 1925, Emma lost her husband. Desolate and conscience-stricken, she confided to Cornélia: "He should have married a woman like you, Nelly: you could have made something of Ernest. He was a very sensitive man but his father quite overshadowed him, and I too dominated him when we were together." She wrote to Sarah Fischer, saying: "Life is no longer the same for me."

Five years later, on April 3, 1930, Emma Lajeunesse left the world in her turn. *La Presse* reported: "Albani died today in London. The illustrious French Canadian songstress was eighty-two. Her health had been fragile for some time." Emma was laid in an open-faced coffin, in her last black silk dress and without any jewellery at all. With her startlingly bare white hands and neck, she evoked a recumbent medieval queen, a marble sculpture in an opera set of a cathedral. The funeral ceremony took place on April 5 at the Church of the Servites in London and was attended by Cornélia, Ernest Frederick, and representatives of the English Royal Family, the Opéra de Paris, Covent Garden Theatre, and other English musical institutions. The Canadian High Commissioner to Britain, former students and colleagues, and devoted fans who had never forgotten her performances also came to pay homage to Albani. The assembly broke into spontaneous applause when the casket was carried into the church – the diva's last dramatic entrance.

Emma and Ernest Gye are buried side-by-side in Brompton Cemetery, London, near the grave of Cornélia Lajeunesse, who died two years after Emma.

As for Ernest Frederick, he lived in Montreal as a British diplomat between 1941 and 1952. He died in 1955, leaving no descendants. A few years before his death, he had instituted the Albani Prize, an annual scholarship awarded every year to a promising young soprano – a fitting tribute to his mother.

Town of Chambly, Albani Archives.

Albani in concert under the direction of Auguste Manns and accompanied by an imposing choir, at the Handel Festival at the Crystal Palace in London, 1900.

Epilogue

In 1926, a few years before the celebrated Canadian soprano's death, a *San Francisco Chronicle* journalist had written: "The first great artist that Canada gave to the world is Emma Albani, and the second is Éva Gauthier. Both are of French blood."

Emma Albani's gravesite in England is overrun by weeds and bracken. However, she has not been completely forgotten, particularly in her home province, where various works of music, theatre, and poetry have been dedicated to her.

Although she has no direct descendants, there is a musical Lajeunesse family connection to popular singer André Lejeune (shortened from Lajeunesse). "We listened to her recordings a lot at home," he remembers. "I was classically trained: my father wanted me to be an opera tenor."

"She was a great-aunt on my father's side," says Dominique Lajeunesse, a well-known Quebec television personality. "Papa, who had a beautiful singing voice, used to say that it ran in the family. A cousin of ours, living in Washington, owns one of Albani's first records. The sound is not very good, but it's one of the last surviving recordings by her, and it's part of the Lajeunesse family heritage."

Albany in one of her opera costumes, circa 1880.

Chronology of Emma Lajeunesse Albani (1847-1930)

Compiled by Michèle Vanasse

EMMA ALBANI AND OPERA

1847
Emma, the first child of Joseph Lajeunesse and Mélina Mignault, is born in Chambly, Quebec. Both her parents are trained musicians.

1849
Emma's sister, Marie Délia (Cornélia, or "Nelly"), is born.

1850
Joseph-Adélard, Emma's younger brother, is born.

CANADA AND THE WORLD

1847
Lord Elgin is named governor of a united Canada. The Union Act joining Upper and Lower Canada has been in force for six years (since 1841).

Agitation in Europe foreshadows democratic and social revolution the following year.

1849
There is rioting in Montreal following the adoption of a law compensating the victims of the Rebellion of 1837-1838.

1850
England under Victoria (crowned in 1837) is at the height of its glory in the second half of the century.

Emma Albani

EMMA ALBANI AND OPERA

Emma's mother begins teaching her the piano.

In Germany, Richard Wagner stages his opera *Lohengrin* in Weimar; it is directed by Franz Liszt.

1851
Giuseppe Verdi's *Rigoletto* triumphs in Venice.

1852
Emma is five when the Lajeunesse family moves to Plattsburg, N.Y. Emma's father takes over her musical training (harp, piano, and voice) until her departure for Europe in 1868.

1856
Emma's mother dies in childbirth; the baby, Mélina, dies soon afterward. The family moves to Montreal. Emma, at eleven, appears onstage as a singer and pianist there and in smaller Quebec towns, including Chambly.

In Germany, Richard Wagner completes *Die Walküre*.

1858
Emma and Cornélia go to study at the Sacred Heart Convent in Sault-au-Récollet (on the north shore of Montreal Island); their

CANADA AND THE WORLD

Its industry, commerce, and wealth give it world dominance. Its political regime, founded on public freedoms and the parliamentary system, is regarded as exemplary.

1851
Louis-Napoléon, elected President of the French Republic in 1848, orchestrates a *coup d'état*; he dismisses the National Assembly and consolidates his personal power.

1852
In France, Louis-Napoléon reestablishes the Empire, adopting the title Napoléon III.

In Piedmont, King Vittorio Emmanuele II calls on Cavour to unite Italy.

1856
In Germany, archaeologists uncover the remains of Neanderthal man, dated 70,000 B.C.

The Crimean War ends; Tsar Alexander II is forced to cede the Crimea to the Turks.

1858
Ottawa is chosen the capital of Canada.

International Star

EMMA ALBANI AND OPERA

father teaches music there. After Emma wins all the school music prizes, she is no longer allowed to compete.

In Paris, Jacques Offenbach presents the comic opera, *Orphée aux Enfers*.

1859
Charles Gounod's opera *Faust* is created at the Théâtre lyrique in Paris.

1860
The Prince of Wales (the future Edward VII) officially inaugurates the Victoria Bridge in Montreal. Emma sings as a soloist with the Montreal Oratorio Society at the ceremony.

1862
With Cornélia, Emma gives a recital at the Mechanics Hall in Montreal. She sings and plays the piano and the harp. The

CANADA AND THE WORLD

The first Canadian currency, minted in England, goes into circulation.

France allies with Piedmont to organize Italy into a confederation.

1859
Napoléon III defeats the Austrians at Solferino in northern Italy. A series of insurrections in favour of a free and united Italy ensue.

1860
Abraham Lincoln is elected President of the United States.

Garibaldi's expedition to Sicily results in the unification of southern Italy with Piedmont. Vittorio Emmanuele II is consecrated ruler of the new kingdom in March 1861.

1861
Tsar Alexander II of Russia passes the Emancipation Act, freeing Russian serfs and giving them ownership of land.

Prince Albert – the Prince Consort, Queen Victoria's husband – dies of typhoid fever.

1862
The Emancipation Act is proclaimed in the U.S. as civil war rages between the Northern states and the South, where the

149

Emma Albani

EMMA ALBANI AND OPERA

newspaper *La Minerve* hails her as a prodigy.

1864
In New York State, Emma gives recitals in Johnstown, Saratoga Springs, and Albany, where the Lajeunesse family settles. Emma is hired as a soloist, then as organist and choir-mistress at St. Joseph's Church.

Gounod's opera *Mireille* has a successful debut in Paris.

1865
Richard Wagner's opera *Tristan und Isolde* is performed for the first time in Munich.

1866
The premieres of Offenbach's opéra-bouffe, *La vie parisienne*, and Georges Bizet's opera, *La jolie fille de Perth*, take place in Paris.

1867
Bishop Conroy of Albany organizes a benefit concert to raise money for Emma to study music in Europe.

Giuseppe Verdi's grand opera *Don Carlos* and Gounod's *Roméo et Juliette* premiere in Paris.

CANADA AND THE WORLD

Confederate Army opposes the end of slavery.

1864
At the Charlottetown and Quebec Conferences, delegates formulate a detailed plan for Canadian union.

In the American West, Native Americans fight to defend their territory.

The First Socialist International takes place in London.

1865
The American Civil War is won by the North; Abraham Lincoln is assassinated by secessionist fanatic John Wilkes Booth.

1866
Prussian Kaiser Wilhelm I and his chancellor, Otto Von Bismarck, devise a confederation of the northern independent states of Germany.

1867
The British North America Act, enacted by the British Parliament, provides for Canadian Confederation, with a distribution of powers between the federal and provincial governments. John A. Macdonald becomes prime minister of the new country.

Garibaldi's March on Rome is halted by French troops.

150

International Star

EMMA ALBANI AND OPERA

1868
In Paris, Emma studies under Gilbert-Louis Duprez, the renowned tenor. Living at the home of the Baroness Laffitte, Emma meets many well-known personalities from the Parisian artistic milieu.

1869
Emma studies singing at the Milan Conservatory with Maestro Francesco Lamperti. She adopts the pseudonym Albani, the name of a patrician Italian family, as her stage name. She sings minor roles in Messina, Sicily before her debut there.

1870
Emma's debut as Amina in Bellini's *La sonnambula* is a huge success in Messina. She is transformed into a diva, adulated by audiences there, and in Acireale, Cento, and Florence. She is engaged to sing for the opera season in Malta. Due to her great success in Malta, she receives an offer to perform in London.

CANADA AND THE WORLD

1868
Thomas D'Arcy McGee, one of the Fathers of Confederation, is assassinated in Ottawa.

The Académie de musique du Québec (AMQ) is founded to raise the level of musical studies in the province.

French Canadian Zouave troops go to Rome to help defend the Vatican against Garibaldi.

1869
Louis Riel leads the Red River Rebellion.

The Suez Canal, linking the Mediterranean and Red Seas and under the direction of French engineer Ferdinand de Lesseps, is officially opened.

1870
Manitoba becomes a Canadian province.

Canadian towns and cities begin to build opera houses to give touring theatre and musical companies places to perform.

Napoléon III falls from power after France's defeat in the Franco-Prussian War. The Republic is declared in Paris.

Rome falls to Garibaldi and becomes the capital of the united kingdom of Italy.

Emma Albani

Emma Albani and Opera

1871
Emma and Cornélia go to London; Emma signs a contract with Frederick Gye of the Covent Garden Theatre for the 1872 opera season. She goes to prepare with Maestro Lamperti in Como, studies *Mignon* with its composer Ambroise Thomas in Paris, and triumphs in that opera in Florence.

Verdi's *Aïda* premieres in Cairo, Egypt.

1872
Joseph Lajeunesse moves to England to be with his daughters.

Emma makes her London debut at Covent Garden in *La sonnambula*. She also sings Donizetti's *Lucia di Lammermoor* and *Linda di Chamounix*, and Gilda in Verdi's *Rigoletto*. She performs for the first time at the English festivals.

Georges Bizet composes the opera *L'Arlésienne*.

In Bayreuth, Bavaria, the cornerstone is laid for the opera festival theatre.

1873
Albani continues to shine at Covent Garden Theatre. In the autumn, she triumphs in Moscow and St. Petersburg, where she sings before Tsar Alexander II.

Canada and the World

1871
The colony of British Columbia votes to join the Dominion of Canada on the promise of a railway link with the East.

In Germany, the German Empire is proclaimed, with Kaiser Wilhem I of Prussia as Emperor.

In France the Paris Commune is suppressed. Adolphe Thiers is named President of the Republic.

1872
Canada legalizes trade unions.

In France, a law is enacted forbidding propaganda from the Socialist International.

1873
Prince Edward Island joins Confederation.

Germany, Russia, and Austria sign the Triple Alliance.

Emma Albani and opera

1874
In January, Albani sings at the wedding of Queen Victoria's second son and Tsar Alexander's only daughter in St. Petersburg. She triumphs at Covent Garden in Bellini's *I puritani*. In July, she is invited to sing for Queen Victoria at Windsor Castle, and a friendship springs up between the two women.

Emma tours the U.S.A.; in New York City, she sings Elsa in Wagner's *Lohengrin* for the first time.

Napoléon Legendre writes the first biography of the diva; entitled *Albani, Emma Lajeunesse*, it is published in Quebec City.

The opera *Boris Godunov* by Modest Mussorgsky premieres in St. Petersburg.

1875
On her return from North America, Albani sings *Lucia di Lammermoor* opposite tenor Francesco Tamagno in Venice, before King Vittorio Emmanuele II and Emperor Franz Josef of Austria.

Wagner's *Lohengrin* has its successful English premiere, at Covent Garden with Albani in the role of Elsa. Emma sings at the Norwich Festival and tours Scotland and Ireland.

Canada and the World

1874
John A. Macdonald is defeated by the Liberals after the Pacific Railway scandal of 1873. The new prime minister is Alexander Mackenzie; Wilfrid Laurier is elected to the House of Commons for the first time.

In Paris, the Impressionist painters hold their first group exhibition.

1875
The Supreme Court of Canada, the highest court of appeal in civil and criminal cases, is created.

In France, the Third Republic is constituted.

The British Parliament acquires majority shares in the Suez Canal Company, strengthening its influence in Egypt.

Emma Albani

Emma Albani and Opera

Bizet's *Carmen* electrifies Paris. The new Paris Opera House (Palais Garnier) is completed.

1876
Albani performs Italian opera in Nice, France. She has a huge success in Wagner's *Tannhäuser* at Covent Garden. She is increasingly in demand as an oratorio singer, performing at the festivals of Birmingham and Leeds.

In August, Wagner's four-part *Ring* cycle is created at the opening of the Bayreuth Festival Theatre.

1877
Albani is engaged for the season at the Théâtre Italien in Paris. She is received and decorated by the President of the French Republic, Patrice de MacMahon.

She sings Senta in Wagner's *Die fliegende Holländer*. She is principal soloist at the Handel Festival held in the Crystal Palace, London.

Camille Saint-Saëns' opera, *Samson et Dalila*, is created at Weimar.

1878
Albani sings a second Paris season, adding the role of Violetta in Verdi's *La traviata* to her repertoire. At Covent Garden, she sings Virginie in Victor Massé's opera, *Paul et Virginie*.

Canada and the World

1876
Indian reserves are instituted in Canada.

Alexander Graham Bell of Tutela Heights, near Brantford, Ontario, invents the telephone and patents it in the U.S.

Queen Victoria assumes the title Empress of India.

1877
Thomas Edison patents the phonograph, or "talking machine," in the U.S.

In South Africa, the British, who control Cape Colony and Natal, annex the Transvaal.

1878
John A. Macdonald is re-elected prime minister of Canada.

In the U.S., Thomas Edison invents the light bulb; electricity begins to transform the cities.

International Star

Emma Albani and Opera

On August 6, Emma marries Ernest Gye, who succeeds his father Frederick as manager of Covent Garden when the latter dies in November.

W.S. Gilbert and Arthur Sullivan produce their first major success, the comic opera *H.M.S. Pinafore*, in London.

1879
On June 4, Ernest Frederick, Emma and Ernest's only child, is born. In the autumn, Emma sings at the Bristol and Hereford festivals; she travels to Florence where she performs in *Faust*, *Rigoletto*, and *Lucia di Lammermoor*.

Tchaikovsky's opera *Eugene Onegin* premieres in Moscow.

1880
Albani gives recitals in Nice and at the Théâtre de la Monnaie in Brussels. She has a rare fiasco in Milan, performing *Lucia di Lammermoor* and *Rigoletto*. She is welcomed warmly on her return to Covent Garden, where she sings *Faust*, *Lucia*, and *Lohengrin*.

1881
Albani gives a benefit performance of *Rigoletto* in Brussels. At Covent Garden, Albani sings Tamara in *The Demon*, directed by its composer, Anton Rubinstein. She tours England, Scotland, and Ireland.

Canada and the World

In Germany, Chancellor Bismarck pushes anti-socialist laws through the Reichstag.

1879
The Casavant Brothers found their organ-making business in Quebec City.

Poet Émile Nelligan is born in Montreal.

Austria-Hungary and Germany create a defensive alliance against Russia.

1880
In Canada, Canadian Pacific president William Van Horne begins laying the trans-Canada railway.

Ferdinand de Lesseps oversees the digging of the Panama Canal.

1881
Under the Bardo Treaty, Tunisia becomes a French protectorate.

Tsar Alexander II is assassinated by a Nihilist in St. Petersburg.

Emma Albani

Emma Albani and Opera

Jacques Offenbach's opéra fantastique, *Les contes d'Hoffman*, premieres in a posthumous tribute performance at the Opéra-Comique in Paris.

1882
Albani sings *Lohengrin* in German in Berlin, and *Rigoletto*, *Faust*, and *Hamlet* in Monte Carlo. At the Birmingham Festival, she takes part in the first performance of Charles Gounod's *Rédemption* under the direction of its composer. He composes the oratorio *Mors et Vita* expressly for Emma.

Wagner's opera *Parsifal* premieres at Bayreuth.

1883
During a North American tour, Emma sings in Montreal. She is treated to a heroine's welcome; a type of hat and a cake are named for her.

Richard Wagner dies in Venice.

The Metropolitan Opera in New York is inaugurated with a performance of Gounod's *Faust*.

1884
At Covent Garden, Albani sings Gounod's *Roméo et Juliette* in Italian and *Lohengrin* in German. She tours Belgium and Holland after the English festival season.

Canada and the World

The British recognize the independence of the Transvaal.

1882
The Triple Alliance of Austria-Hungary, Germany, and Italy is formed to isolate France in case of war.

Egypt becomes a British protectorate.

1883
Karl Marx, philosopher and author of *Capital* and *The Communist Manifesto*, dies in London.

The Russian Communist Party is founded.

The Orient Express, the luxury train service from London to Istanbul, is inaugurated.

1884
The daily newspaper *La Presse* is founded in Montreal.

In France, professional unions win legal recognition and the right to strike.

International Star

EMMA ALBANI AND OPERA

Queen Victoria visits the Gyes at their Scottish vacation home.

Jules Massenet's most successful opera, *Manon*, premieres in Paris.

1885
Albani sings at the Handel Festival in London (the *Messiah*), and at the Birmingham Festival with triumphant success in Gounod's *Mors et Vita*, and Antonín Dvořák's cantata, *The Spectre's Bride*.

1886
Albani performs in Holland, then returns to London to sing Liszt's oratorio, *The Legend of St. Elisabeth*, directed by the composer.

At Leeds, she interprets two new works: Arthur Sullivan's *The Golden Legend*, and Dvořák's cantata, *St. Ludmila*.

1887
At the Royal Opera House in Berlin, Emma sings *Lohengrin* and *Die fliegande Holländer* in German; she also performs in

CANADA AND THE WORLD

1885
The Last Spike ceremony at Craigellachie, British Columbia, symbolizes the completion of the Canadian Pacific Railway (CPR) across Canada.

Fearing to lose their land, Métis and Indians under Louis Riel in Saskatchewan rebel against the Canadian government. Riel's hanging for treason creates an irresolvable problem for Canadian unity.

1886
The first through passenger train on the CPR arrives in Port Moody, B.C. on July 4; completion of the railway allows entertainers to travel more economically and quickly.

The Berlin Conference carves up Africa, dividing it among the European powers.

The Statue of Liberty is unveiled, a monument to French-American friendship.

1887
The election of Honoré Mercier as the premier of Quebec reflects a growing French Canadian nationalism.

Emma Albani

EMMA ALBANI AND OPERA

Rigoletto, *La traviata*, and *Faust* (in Italian). She tours Belgium, Holland, England, Scotland, and Ireland.

Verdi's *Otello* premieres at La Scala in Milan.

1888
Albani gives concerts in Norway, Sweden, and Denmark, then tours Belgium and Holland.

Édouard Lalo's *Le roi d'Ys* premieres in Paris.

1889
Albani tours Canada; she and Ernest are the guests of Sir John A. Macdonald and Honoré Mercier. She sings in San Francisco for the first time. In London, Emma sings *Faust* for the Shah of Persia. She tours the U.S.A. and Mexico.

1890
Albani returns to Canada to sing *Lucia* and *La traviata*. She gives a concert in aid of the Notre-Dame Hospital in Montreal.

Alexander Borodin's opera, *Prince Igor*, is created in St. Petersburg.

CANADA AND THE WORLD

Queen Victoria's Golden Jubilee celebrates the fiftieth year of her reign.

Emile Berliner invents the gramophone. His company, Berliner Gramophone, is the first to produce musical recordings; it later becomes RCA Victor.

1888
While European immigration is being encouraged to develop agriculture in the Canadian West, Premier Honoré Mercier begins an aggressive land colonization scheme in Quebec.

Kaiser Wilhelm II succeeds his father as German Emperor.

1889
The Eiffel Tower is built for the Paris World's Fair.

Twenty-three countries found the Second Socialist International in Paris.

Japan adopts a constitution by which ministers are accountable only to the Emperor; it will remain in effect until 1945.

1890
At Wounded Knee, South Dakota, the Sioux under Big Foot are massacred by the U.S. cavalry.

International Star

EMMA ALBANI AND OPERA

1891
Albani performs before Emperor Wilhelm II during his official visit to Britain. She sings *Otello* at Covent Garden and *Rigoletto* at the Metropolitan Opera in New York City.

1892
Emma sings the whole season at the Met in New York (Gounod's *Faust*, Mozart's *Don Giovanni*, Meyerbeer's *Les Huguenots*, and Wagner's *Lohengrin*, *Die fliegende Holländer*, and *Die Meistersinger*); in Montreal, she performs *Les Huguenots* and *Lohengrin*.

I pagliacci by Ruggero Leoncavallo premieres in Milan.

1893
Emma sings at Covent Garden and at the English festivals. She tours Austria, Hungary, and Bohemia. In Vienna, she sings excerpts from Brahm's *Requiem* in the presence of the composer.

Verdi's last opera, *Falstaff*, is created at La Scala, and Puccini's *Manon Lescaut* premieres in Turin.

CANADA AND THE WORLD

1891
The first cinema camera, called the kinetograph, is patented by Thomas Edison and William Dickson.

In Russia, the construction of the Trans-Siberian railway begins.

Canada's prime minister, Sir John A. Macdonald, dies in office.

1892
France and Russia join in a pact in the eventuality of war with Germany.

Actress Sarah Bernhardt takes audiences by storm in Europe and North America.

1893
The Monument national theatre is built in Montreal.

Henry Ford puts the first motor car on the road in the U.S.

In France, legislators are accused of corruption in the Panama scandal.

159

Emma Albani

Emma Albani and Opera

1894
Albani tours Germany and visits Ernest Frederick who is at school in Geneva, Switzerland.

1895
Albani opens the season at Covent Garden, singing Desdemona in *Otello*. She creates the role of Edith in *Harold*, a new opera by English composer, Frederick Cowan.

1896
In January, Albani sings at the Monument national theatre in Montreal.

Albani sings her last season at Covent Garden. She triumphs as Isolde (in German) and performs the role of Donna Anna in *Don Giovanni* for the first time.

She undertakes a trans-Canada tour.

The premiere of Puccini's *La bohème* takes place in Turin.

Canada and the World

1894
The Pathé brothers open the first French phonograph and record factory.

Canadian poet and entertainer Pauline Johnson sails to England to find a publisher. Later in the year, she tours western Canada with her partner, travelling by train to the West Coast.

1895
Alfred Dreyfus, a Jewish army officer convicted of espionage, is sent into exile; his trial has divided France into two camps.

The Lumière brothers, inventors of the *cinématographe*, present the first moving picture show to the public at the Grand Café in Paris.

1896
The Liberals under Wilfrid Laurier take power in Ottawa. Laurier is the first prime minister of French Canadian ancestry.

Canada experiences a period of prosperity; the population increases due to a policy of bringing European immigrants to farm in Western Canada.

In Quebec, the pulp and paper, mining, and hydroelectricity industries are booming.

International Star

EMMA ALBANI AND OPERA

1897
Emma Albani, together with pianist Jan Paderewski, is awarded the gold Beethoven medal by the Royal Philharmonic Society of London.

1898
Albani tours Australia and South Africa for the first time.

1899
Albani sings *Lohengrin* for Queen Victoria at Windsor Castle. She returns to South Africa for a second performance tour.

Jules Massenet presents his opera version of *Cendrillon* (Cinderella) at the Opéra-Comique in Paris.

1900
Puccini's *Tosca* premieres in Rome on January 14.

CANADA AND THE WORLD

1897
Queen Victoria's Diamond Jubilee celebrates the sixtieth year of her reign.

Guglielmo Marconi establishes the first wireless communication.

Englishman Joseph John Thomson discovers the presence of electrons in the atom.

Theodor Herzl founds the Zionist movement with the objective of creating a Jewish state in Palestine.

1898
The U.S. establishes a protectorate over Cuba and the Hawaiian Islands.

1899
Canada sends troops to fight for England in the Boer War in South Africa.

Quebec nationalist leader Henri Bourassa opposes Canadian participation in the wars of the British Empire.

A Church-led union movement begins in Quebec.

1900
The World's Fair in Paris is a showcase for new technological developments.

161

Emma Albani

Emma Albani and Opera

1901
Albani sings excerpts from Handel's *Messiah* at Queen Victoria's funeral ceremony.

1902
Emma sings at the coronation of Edward VII.

Claude Debussy's opera, *Pelléas et Mélisande*, premieres in Paris.

1903
On tour in Canada, Albani sings in Montreal, Three Rivers, and Sherbrooke; she receives mixed reviews.

1904
Emma Albani records for the first time in London.

Joseph Lajeunesse dies in Chambly.

Emma tours South Africa a third time.

The premiere of Puccini's *Madama Butterfly* is a resounding failure at La Scala.

Canada and the World

1901
Queen Victoria dies at age eighty-two.

Marconi succeeds in transmitting messages by wireless telegraphy between Cornwall, England and St. John's, Newfoundland.

1902
The Boer War ends.

Theodore Roosevelt becomes President of the United States.

The violent Irish nationalist movement Sinn Fein is founded.

1903
The Grand Trunk Company builds a second transcontinental railway line across Canada.

Henry Ford founds the Ford Motor Company.

1904
Roosevelt instigates the "big stick" policy to protect American interests in Latin America.

France and England join in the *Entente cordiale* in response to the German-Austrian-Italian Triple Alliance.

International Star

EMMA ALBANI AND OPERA

1905
Richard Strauss' opera *Salome* premieres in Dresden, Germany.

1906
Albani gives her farewell tour of Canada. She sings in Montreal for the last time, performing excerpts from *Tannhäuser* at the Mount Royal Arena on April 9. Her last Canadian concert is given in Ottawa two days later, before Sir Wilfrid Laurier.

1907
Emma, now sixty years old, tours Australia, New Zealand, India, and Ceylon.

She tours North America with Quebec pianist Emiliano Renaud.

Performances of *Salome*, decried as improper, are cancelled at the Met in New York.

CANADA AND THE WORLD

1905
Alberta and Saskatchewan become provinces of Canada.

The provincial Liberal Party under Jean-Lomer Gouin is elected in Quebec.

1906
The Ouimetoscope, the first movie-house in Montreal, opens on St. Catherine St.

Dreyfus is pardoned and rehabilitated in France.

On her second trip to England, Pauline Johnson, "the Mohawk Princess," performs in both public recitals and private salons and develops new markets for her writing.

San Francisco is devastated by an earthquake and fire.

In Russia, the Douma, a parliament of elected representatives, is established following a series of strikes and peasant revolts.

1907
The first images are transmitted between Paris and London by cable.

Cultural programs called "chautauquas" are popular in communities in the U.S. and Canada. Pauline Johnson makes a gruelling ten-week tour of the American

Emma Albani

EMMA ALBANI AND OPERA	CANADA AND THE WORLD
	plains states as part of the chautauqua circuit.

1911
Emma gives her farewell performance at the Royal Albert Hall in London on October 14. She publishes her memoirs, *Forty Years of Song*, in London. Although retired, she occasionally performs for charitable causes.

Igor Stravinsky composes the score of the ballet *Petrushka*.

1914
Emma sings Bellini's *I puritani* in a private performance and gives recitals to aid the war effort. Ernest's unlucky investments land the couple in a difficult financial situation. Emma is obliged to sell her opera costumes, her jewellery and art objects.

1911
Robert Borden, Progressive Conservative, is elected prime minister of Canada.

King George V is crowned in England.

Norwegian explorer Roald Amundsen reaches the South Pole.

1914
The First World War begins after Archduke Ferdinand of Austria-Hungary is shot by a Serb in Sarajevo. Austria and Germany are ranged against Russia, France, and Great Britain. Canada supports Great Britain and sends troops to the front.

1917
The October (Bolshevik) Revolution in Russia deposes the monarchy.

Conscription divides Canadians along French/English lines.

1918
On November 11, an armistice ends the First World War.

The worldwide influenza epidemic kills almost twenty-two million people in two years.

International Star

Emma Albani and opera

1920
The British Government grants an annual pension of £100 to Emma Albani. The money earned by giving singing lessons and by selling her most valuable mementoes is not enough to meet her needs.

1925
The Canadian federal government and the Quebec provincial government both deny a pension to Albani. Benefit concerts are organized for her in London, Montreal, and Chambly.

George V confers the title of Dame Commander of the British Empire on Albani, with an accompanying annual pension of £300.

Emma's husband, Ernest, dies.

Canada and the World

In Canada, all women (except status Indians) are eligible to vote in federal elections.

In Britain, women over thirty get the vote.

1920
The Roaring Twenties begin; the decade is characterized by a spirit of carefree materialism. New household labour-saving appliances, cars, and radios bring more leisure to those who can enjoy it.

1921
Agnes Macphail is the first woman elected to Parliament in Canada. William Lyon Mackenzie King becomes prime minister.

1922
The Union of Soviet Socialist Republics (U.S.S.R.) is formed from the Russian empire.

1925
Aldolf Hitler publishes *Mein Kampf*, a glorification of German hegemony.

The Fascist Party becomes the only legal political party in Italy, and Mussolini obtains unlimited powers.

Germany, France, Great Britain, Italy, Belgium, Poland, and Czechoslovakia sign the Treaty of Locarno, guaranteeing the borders established by the Treaty of Versailles

165

Emma Albani and Opera

Canada and the World

(1918) and agreeing to submit cases of conflict to arbitration.

1927
The Jazz Singer is the first talking movie to appear on the screen.

1928
West Coast artist Emily Carr exhibits her work in central Canada, establishing herself as a major artist.

To earn money during Parliament's summer recess, Agnes Macphail, MP makes a ten-week speaking tour of western Canada as part of the chautauqua circuit.

1929
With the collapse of the U.S. Stock Exchange in October, the ten-year-long Great Depression begins.

1930
On April 3, Emma Albani dies in London. She is buried there, next to Ernest. Her sister and loyal friend Cornélia dies two years later.

The City of Montreal names a street in Albani's honour, and Chambly names its parish hall after her. Other municipalities follow suit.

1934
Ernest Frederick Gye creates the annual Albani Prize, to be awarded

1930
The French begin to build the Maginot Line of defence along the Franco-German border to protect Alsace and Lorraine against a German invasion.

In Canada, the Conservatives under R.B. Bennett defeat Mackenzie King's Liberals to win the federal election.

1934
The Dionne quintuplets are born in Callendar, Ontario.

Emma Albani and Opera

by the London Conservatory of Music to a promising young soprano.

1938
A biography of Emma Albani, entitled *L'Albani, sa carrière artistique et triomphale*, by Hélène Charbonneau, is published in Montreal.

1939
A commemorative plaque honouring Emma Albani is placed on the home of her birth in Chambly.

During the ensuing decade, some of Albani's recordings are reissued in the U.S.

Canada and the World

1935
In Canada, Mackenzie King leads the Liberals back to power in a landslide election. Tommy Douglas of the Co-operative Commonwealth Federation (CCF) is elected for the first time.

1938
Hoping to avoid open war with Hitler, France and England accept the Nazis' annexation of Sudetenland by signing the Munich Agreement.

1939
The Second World War begins when France and Britain declare war on Germany after Hitler's invasion of Poland.

Canada declares war on Germany.

The U.S. remains neutral while supplying arms to the Allies.

1941
Japan bombs Pearl Harbor on December 7; the U.S., Canada, and Great Britain declare war on Japan.

1945
Germany surrenders on May 8; the U.S. drops atomic bombs on Japan on August 6 and 9. Japan surrenders on September 2.

Emma Albani

EMMA ALBANI AND OPERA

1955
Ernest Frederick Gye dies in London at age seventy-six after a career in the British Foreign Office. At his death, all documents pertaining to Albani are sent to the Mayor of Chambly, Robert Lebel, who personally covers the postal fees ($400) that the Town of Chambly refuses to pay.

CANADA AND THE WORLD

1951
In Canada, the Massey Commission recommends greater government support of the arts through creation of an arts funding body.

1955
The Eastern Bloc countries under Soviet hegemony join in the Warsaw Pact.

Egyptian President Nasser stops Israeli ships from passing through the Suez Canal, causing skirmishes between Egyptian and Israeli troops.

1957
John Diefenbaker is elected prime minister of Canada.

The Canada Council is established to encourage the study, production, and enjoyment of the arts and social sciences.

1960
In Quebec, Jean Lesage and his Liberals defeat the Union Nationale, and the Quiet Revolution begins.

In the U.S., John F. Kennedy becomes president.

1963
Lester Pearson becomes prime minister of Canada.

International Star

EMMA ALBANI AND OPERA

1967
In celebration of Canada's Centennial Year, eight of Albani's recordings, made in London between 1904 and 1907, are re-released by Rococo, a Toronto recording house.

CANADA AND THE WORLD

1967
The World's Fair, Expo 67, is held during the summer in Montreal as part of Canada's Centennial festivities. President Charles De Gaulle of France visits Canada and shouts *"Vive le Québec libre!"* in Montreal.

Israel defeats Egypt in the Six-Day War.

1968
Pierre Elliott Trudeau succeeds Lester Pearson as leader of the Liberal party and prime minister of Canada. He calls a June election, and "Trudeaumania" takes the country by storm; Canada becomes officially bilingual.

René Lévesque founds the Parti Québécois.

1970
In Canada, Prime Minister Trudeau invokes the War Measures Act during the FLQ crisis.

1972
Musicologist Gilles Potvin publishes an annotated French-language translation of Albani's memoirs, *Forty Years of Song*.

Les Éditions Albani is founded in Chambly.

1972
The Watergate scandal erupts in Washington.

U.S. President Nixon visits China.

1980
Canada Post issues a commemorative stamp for the fiftieth anniversary of Emma Albani's death.

1980
The first Quebec referendum on sovereignty-association with Canada fails to pass.

Emma Albani

EMMA ALBANI AND OPERA

Robert Lebel deposits the Albani papers in the public archives of the Town of Chambly.

1991
At the Théâtre populaire du Québec, young playwright Simon Fortin presents *Le pays dans la gorge*. The main characters are Emma and Cornélia Lajeunesse, Queen Victoria, and Éva Gauthier.

1992
The Montreal recording company Analekta reissues Albani's recording of "Souvenirs du jeune âge" by Ferdinand Hérold in *Les grandes voix du Canada, Vol.1*.

1994
The Country in Her Throat, the English version of Simon Fortin's play about Albani, is directed by Bill Glassco at the Tarragon Theatre in Toronto. Lally Cadeau plays Emma, and Frances Hyland plays Queen Victoria.

1995
A concert in honour of Albani is held at the Château Ramezay Museum in Montreal.

1998
Le pays dans la gorge is revived at the Théâtre du Rideau Vert in Montreal. Emma is played by Isabelle Miquelon, Queen Victoria by Janine Sutto, and Cornélia by singer Louise Forestier.

CANADA AND THE WORLD

Pierre Elliott Trudeau is re-elected prime minister of Canada.

1991
NATO forces defeat Iraq in the Gulf War.

Boris Yeltsin is elected prime minister of Russia by universal suffrage, a first in that country.

1992
The Charlottetown Constitutional Accord is rejected in a pan-Canadian referendum.

1995
The second Quebec sovereignty referendum is defeated by less than a percentage point.

Bibliography/Discography

ALBANI, Emma. *Forty Years of Song*. London: Mills and Boon Ltd., 1911.
– in French: *Mémoires, Emma Albani. L'éblouissante carrière de la plus grande cantatrice québécoise*. Translated and annotated, with chronology, discography, and bibliography, by musicologist Gilles Potvin. Montréal: Éditions du jour, 1972.
ANALEKTA (recording company). *Les grandes voix du Canada, Vol. 1*. Montreal: 1992.
CHARBONNEAU, Hélène. *L'Albani, sa carrière artistique et triomphale*. Montreal: Imprimerie Jacques Cartier, 1938.
FORTIN, Simon. *The Country in Her Throat*. Victoria: Scirocco Drama, 1994.
HOLDEN, Amanda, with Nicholas KENYON and Stephen WALSH. *The Penguin Opera Guide*. London: Penguin Books, 1995.
KALLMAN, Helmut, Gilles POTVIN and Kenneth WINTERS, editors. *Encyclopedia of Music in Canada*. Toronto: University of Toronto Press, 1981.
LOW, Will Hicock. *A Chronicle of Friendships, 1873-1903*. New York: Charles Scribner & Sons, 1908.

MacDonald, Cheryl. *Emma Albani, Victorian Diva.* Toronto: Dundurn Press, 1984.

Pipes, Richard. *Russia under the Old Regime.* London: Weidenfeld & Nicolson, 1974.

Rosenthal, Harold. *Two Centuries of Opera at Covent Garden.* London: Putnam, 1958.

Shaw, George Bernard. *How to Become a Music Critic.* London: Rupert Hart-Davis, 1960.

Shirmer, G. Inc. *The Prima Donna's Album.* New York: 1856.

Strachey, Lytton. *Queen Victoria.* London: Chatto and Windus, 1951.

Troyat, Henri. *La Vie quotidienne en Russia au temps du dernier tsar.* Paris: Hachette, 1959.

Index

Acireale, 54, 55, 58, 151
Albany, N.Y., 35-38, 50, 87-90, 97, 150
Albert, Prince (Victoria's husband), 3-6, 15, 126, 133, 149
Albert Edward (Prince of Wales, later King Edward VII), 31, 33, 81, 108, 133, 137, 149
Alexander II, Tsar, 9, 12, 13, 72, 75-84, 105, 106, 108, 148, 152, 153, 155
Alexandrovna, Princess Marie, 12, 76, 80, 153
Alfred, Duke of Edinburgh, 12, 80, 153
Augusta, Empress (of Germany), 110

Balmoral Castle, 119, 120
Beethoven, Ludwig van, 15, 19, 36
Bellini, Vincenzo, 50, 54, 132
Benedict, Sir Julius, 95
Benoist, François, 43
Berlin, Germany, 77, 110, 111, 121, 156, 157
Bernhardt, Sarah, 24 (n.), 108
Biddulph, Sir Thomas, 6, 7, 17
Bismarck, Otto von, 44, 150, 155
Bologna, Italy, 5, 56
Bourdon, Louis, 110
Bourget, Ignace (Bishop), 28
Brahms, Johannes, 120, 121
Brignoli, Pasquale (tenor), 36
Brussels, 107, 155
Bülow, Hans von, 94

Calgary, Alberta., 129
Calvé, Emma (soprano), 137

Canada, 67, 79, 104, 112, 118, 121, 124, 135, 136, 141, 145
Canadian Pacific Railway, 122, 155, 157
Caruso, Enrico (tenor), 132
Catania, Sicily, 54, 55
Cavalieri, Lina (soprano), 132
Cento, Italy, 55, 151
Chambly, Quebec, 5, 10, 15, 20, 21, 23-26, 29, 30, 51, 104, 115, 126, 128, 134, 135, 137, 141, 147, 162, 165-169
Cipriani, Duchessa di, 53, 54
Como, Italy, 63, 64
Conroy, John J. (Bishop), 36, 37, 39, 150
Covent Garden Theatre (Royal Italian Opera), 5, 17, 46, 60, 62, 65-68, 70, 74, 91, 93, 94, 96, 103, 107-109, 117, 118, 121, 123, 124, 128, 143, 152-156, 159, 160
Crawford, Mr.(impresario and singer), 25
Crystal Palace, London, 99, 120, 144, 154
Cullen, Maurice, 137

Debussy, Claude, 40, 132
Donizetti, Gaetano, 54
Duprez, Gilbert Louis, 41-45, 69, 70, 151
Dvořák, Antonín, 94, 157

Errol, Lady, 3, 7, 12, 15
Eugénie, Empress (of France), 14, 41, 61, 71, 76

173

First World War (Great War), 139, 164
Fischer, Sarah, 141, 142
Florence, Italy, 54-57, 64-66, 107, 151, 155
Flotow, Friedrich von, 35
Forty Years of Song (Albani's memoirs), 138, 164; French translation, 169
France, 39, 43, 59, 61, 97, 128, 149, 151-153, 156
Franz Josef, Emperor (of Austria), 93, 153
Fréchette, Louis-Honoré, 114, 128, 133
Frederika, Crown Princess, 111, 112

Garden, Mary (soprano), 132
Garibaldi, Giuseppe, 59, 149-151
Gauthier, Éva (soprano), 135, 145
George V, King (of England), 130, 141, 142
Germany, 44, 94, 126, 148, 150, 155
Giordano, Umberto, 132, 132 (n.)
Glinka, Mikhail, 121
Gounod, Charles, 15, 46, 112, 120, 124, 149, 150
Graziani, Francesco (baritone), 93
Grisi, Giuletta (soprano), 68
Gye, Ernest (husband), 69, 88, 91, 92, 102, 105, 106, 108, 110, 112-114, 116, 118, 121, 122, 126-128, 134, 136, 137, 139, 142, 143, 155, 164-166
Gye, Ernest Frederick (son), 102, 107, 119, 126-128, 134, 137, 139, 142, 143, 155, 160, 166, 168
Gye, Frederick, 60, 62, 63, 65-67, 88, 91, 94, 103, 106, 152, 155

Her Majesty's Theatre (London), 58, 61

Hérold, Ferdinand, 115
Hugo, Victor, 70
Hummel, Johann, 36

Ireland, 4, 95, 153, 155
Italy, 44, 52, 64, 66, 107, 149

Janáček, Leos, 132

Key, Sir Cooper and Lady Francis, 58
King, William Lyon McKenzie, 141, 166, 167

Labelle, Ludger, 34
Lablache, Louis, 15
Laffitte, Baroness de, 40, 41, 45, 51, 69
Lajeunesse, Adelard (brother), 22, 26, 29, 85, 115, 134, 147
Lajeunesse, Cornélia (sister), 29, 34, 35, 37, 38, 39, 45, 49, 51-54, 56, 58, 61, 64, 67-70, 72, 73, 75, 76, 81, 82, 84, 85, 88, 89, 92, 96, 97, 103-105, 108, 110, 116, 126, 131, 134-137, 139, 142, 143, 147, 148, 152, 166
Lajeunesse, Dominique, 145
Lajeunesse, Emma (Albani)
  acting talent, 23, 28, 29
  adoption of name Albani, 50, 51
  Albani Prize, 143, 166
  benefit nights, 55, 56, 58, 69, 82, 84
  biographies of, 91, 153, 167
  birth, 5, 147
  boarder at Sacred Heart Convent, 26-29, 148, 149
  British pensions, 140, 142, 165
  charity concerts, 58, 124, 164
  compositions, 28, 34, 36
  Covent Garden debut, 65-67
  Dame Commander of the British Empire (DBE), 142, 165

death and funeral, 142, 143, 166
debut (Messina), 50-52, 151
farewell performance (London), 137
first English festival performance, 69
first public performances, 24, 25, 31, 34, 149, 150
fundraising concerts (for musical studies), 34, 35, 37, 150
gala benefits for, 141, 142, 165
holidays in Scotland, 118-120, 157
introduction to Queen Victoria, 9-17
marriage and birth of son, 103-107, 155
marriage proposals to, 38
Metropolitan Opera debut, 126
opera roles:
  Adèle in *Le comte Ory* (Rossini), 56, 64
  Amelia in *Un ballo in maschera* (Verdi), 51
  Amina in *La sonnambula* (Bellini), 15, 21, 50-52, 56, 57, 66, 69, 75, 88, 96, 151, 152
  Antonida in *A Life for the Tsar* (Glinka), 121
  Catherine in *Les Diamants de la couronne* (Auber), 70
  Countess Almaviva in *Les nozze di Figaro* (Mozart), 70, 93
  Desdemona in *Otello* (Verdi), 124-126, 159, 160
  Donna Anna in *Don Giovanni* (Mozart), 160
  Elisabeth in *Tannhäuser* (Wagner), 74, 94, 95, 106, 154, 163
  Elsa in *Lohengrin* (Wagner), 85, 89, 90, 94, 97, 110, 111, 118, 121, 126, 132, 153, 155, 156, 157, 159, 161
  Elvira in *Don Giovanni* (Mozart), 126, 159
  Elvira in *I Puritani* (Bellini), 96, 138, 153, 164
  Eva in *Die Meistersinger* (Wagner), 126, 159
  Gilda in *Rigoletto* (Verdi), 42, 55, 68-71, 75, 77, 88, 93, 96, 99, 121, 152, 155, 156, 159
  Inès in *L'Africaine* (Meyerbeer), 57
  Isabella in *Robert le diable* (Meyerbeer), 57
  Isolde in *Tristan und Isolde* (Wagner), 128, 160
  Juliette in *Roméo et Juliette* (Gounod), 93, 156
  Lady Harriet/Martha in *Martha* (Von Flotow), 35, 57, 68
  Linda in *Linda di Chamounix* (Donizetti), 68, 152
  Lucia in *Lucia di Lammermoor* (Donizetti), 57, 68-70, 75, 88, 96, 107, 124, 152, 153, 155, 158
  Marguerite in *Faust* (Gounod), 42, 43, 46, 93, 106, 121, 126, 128, 155, 156, 158, 159
  Mignon in *Mignon* (Thomas), 64, 65, 88, 89
  Norma in *Norma* (Bellini), 21, 62
  Ophelia in *Hamlet* (Thomas), 70, 75, 79, 156
  Rosina in *Il barbiere di Siviglia* (Rossini), 57
  Senta in *Die fleigende Holländer* (Wagner), 98, 121, 126, 154, 157, 159

175

Tamara in *The Demon* (Rubinstein), 46, 110, 155
Valentine in *Les Huguenots* (Meyerbeer), 126, 159
Violetta in *La traviata* (Verdi) 99, 106, 121, 124, 154, 158
Zerlina in *Don Giovanni* (Mozart), 96
musical training with father, 21-24, 33, 34, 43, 68, 85
musical training with Francesco Lamperti, 41-45, 151
musical training with Louis-Gilbert Duprez, 41-45, 151
oratorio and cantata performances:
  Alma Incantarice (Flotow), 99
  Alma Virgo (Hummel), 36
  Birmingham Festival, 112, 120, 154, 156, 157
  Golden Legend, The (Sullivan), 157
  Handel Festival (London), 99, 120, 133, 144, 154, 157
  Hymn of Praise (Mendelssohn), 95
  Leeds Festival, 154, 157
  Legend of St. Cecilia, The (Benedict), 95
  Legend of St. Elisabeth, The (Liszt), 120, 157
  Liverpool Festival, 87
  Messiah (Handel), 99, 157, 162
  Mors et Vita (Gounod), 120, 156, 157
  Norwich Festival, 95, 153
  Rédemption (Gounod), 112, 156
  Requiem (Brahms), 121, 159
  Spectre's Bride, The (Dvořák), 157
  St. Ludmila (Dvořák), 157

Stabat Mater (Rossini), 25
Theodora (Handel), 95
organist in Albany, 36
performance tours:
  Australia and New Zealand, 135, 163
  Austria, Hungary, and Bohemia, 121, 126, 159
  Belgium and Holland, 156, 158
  Canada, 128, 129, 158, 160, 162;
  farewell tour of Canada, 135, 136, 163
  first American tour, 87-91, 153
  first tour of Ireland and England, 95
  Germany, 110-112, 127, 160
  India and Ceylon, 135, 163
  last Canadian concert, 163
  last North American tour, 163
  Montreal, 126, 134, 160
  Russia, 73-85, 105-106, 152, 153
  Scotland and Ireland, 158
  second North American tour, 112-115, 156
  second tour of South Africa, 135, 161
  South Africa and Australia, 132, 161
  third North American tour, 121, 122, 158
  third tour of South Africa, 162
  U.S. and Mexico, 124, 158
publication of memoirs, 138, 164
recordings, 112, 145, 162, 167, 169, 170
reviews and comments in newspapers
  Albany Argus, 89
  Albany Morning Express, 89

Berliner Zeitung, 111
Daily Telegraph (London), 108
Gazzetta di Messina, 52
Hamilton Spectator, 129
Il Corriere Siciliano, 55
La France, 70
La Minerve (Montreal), 34, 50
La Presse (Montreal), 134, 142
L'Ordre (Quebec), 34
Musical Times (London), 67
New York Herald Tribune, 89
Republic (New York), 90
San Francisco Chronicle, 145
The Times (London), 111
Troy Daily Times, 35
sings at Victoria's funeral, 133, 162
sings for Prince of Wales (Montreal), 33
soloist at St. Joseph's Church, Albany, 36-38
Lajeunesse, Joseph (father), 9, 21-25, 28, 33, 37, 38, 52-54, 56, 67, 70, 85, 92, 93, 101, 104, 114, 115, 126, 128, 134, 147, 148, 152
Lajeunesse, Mélina, née Mignault (mother), 10, 19, 21-23, 26, 27, 105, 147, 148
Lamperti, Francesco, 44, 47-51, 56, 63-65, 151, 152
La Scala (Milan), 49, 107, 159
Laurier, Sir Wilfrid, 135, 136, 153, 159, 160, 163,
Lavigne family, 23, 24
Legendre, Napoléon (biographer), 91, 153
Lejeune, André, 145
Les Éditions Albani (Chambly), 169
Lind, Jenny (soprano), 56, 71
Liszt, Franz, 94, 120, 121, 148

Livingstone, David, 68, 72
London, England, 5, 10, 59, 61-65, 68, 87, 93, 94, 99-104, 106, 108-111, 120, 122, 128, 136-138, 140-142, 150-152, 154, 157, 158, 161, 162, 164-166, 169
Low, Will Hicock (artist), 97, 98
Lucca, Pauline (soprano), 64

Macdonald, Sir John A., 122, 150, 153, 154, 158, 159
MacMahon, Patrice de, 97, 154
Malta, 10, 12, 57, 58, 61, 66, 71, 151
Mapleson, James Henry, 58, 61
Marchesi, Matilde (soprano), 137
Margherita, Queen (of Italy), 93
Martin, Jean Blaise, 40
McCrea (Colonel), 58, 61, 71
Mechanics' Hall (Montreal), 24, 34, 149
Melba, Nelly (soprano), 123, 137, 141, 142
Mendelssohn, Felix, 15, 95
Mercier, Honoré (Premier of Quebec), 122, 157, 158
Messina, Sicily, 10, 49-54, 66, 151
Mexico City, 124
Meyerbeer, Giacomo, 128
Mignault, Rachel, née McKutcheon (maternal grandmother), 15, 19, 23, 26, 29, 30, 115
Mignault, Rose Délima (aunt), 23, 29
Milan, Italy, 14, 44, 47, 49, 51, 107, 108, 110, 151, 155, 159
Miolan-Carvalho, Caroline (soprano), 64, 68
Montreal, Quebec, 23, 25, 31, 34, 113-115, 122, 124, 126, 134, 135, 137, 148, 155, 156, 158, 160, 162, 163, 165-167, 170, 171

177

Emma Albani

Montreal Oratorio Society, 31, 149
Monument national (Montreal), 135, 159
Moscow, Russia, 72, 73, 75-77, 105, 152, 155
Mozart, W. A., 36, 128
Munich, Germany, 94, 150
Mussorgsky, Modest, 82, 153

Napoléon III, Emperor (of France), 14, 44, 61, 71, 148, 149, 151
New York Academy of Music, 85, 88, 89
New York City, 87-91, 113, 126, 127, 153, 159, 163
Novello, Clara (soprano), 99

Old Mar Lodge, Scotland, 118, 119
Ottawa, Ontario, 122, 135, 136, 163

Paris, France, 14, 32, 39, 40, 43-45, 61, 65, 69, 70, 77, 96, 97, 99, 100, 124, 149-154, 156, 158, 161, 162,
Patti, Adelina (soprano), 36, 64, 68, 70-72, 113, 124, 136, 137
Pays dans la gorge, Le (play by Simon Fortin), 170 ; English translation/production, *The Country in Her Throat*, 170
Philadelphia, Pa., 87, 91
Plattsburgh, N.Y., 19, 148
Poniatowski, Prince, 41, 44, 47
Prokofiev, Sergei, 132

Quebec, province of, 37, 84, 114, 146, 157
Quebec City, 121, 127, 146, 153, 155
Queen's Hall (Montreal), 114, 115

Reszke, Jean de (tenor), 124, 125
Rossini, Gioachino, 25, 41, 140
Rubinstein, Anton, 46, 110, 155
Russia, 12, 13, 72, 77, 105, 108, 152, 155

Sacred Heart Convent, 26, 27-30, 33, 115, 148
Saratoga Springs, N.Y., 35, 150
Sargent, John Singer (artist), 99
Scotland, 4, 102, 118-120, 153, 158
Shah of Persia, 81, 122, 123, 158
Shaw, George Bernard, 123-125
Sicily, 50, 54, 55
Stanley, Henry, 68, 72
St. Petersburg, Russia, 13, 72, 75-77, 80, 83, 84, 106, 108, 110, 121, 152, 155, 158
Strakosch, Maurice, 36, 44, 45, 88
Strakosch, Max, 88-91
Strauss, Richard, 132, 163
Stravinsky, Igor, 132, 164
Sullivan, Sir Arthur, 120, 137, 155
Switzerland, 127, 160

Tamagno, Francesco (tenor), 92, 124, 153
Taschereau, Alexandre, 141
Teatro della Fenice (Venice), 92
Teatro della Pergola (Florence), 65
Teatro Politeama (Florence), 56
Théâtre Italien (Paris), 96, 100, 154
Théâtre St. Denis (Montreal), 141
Thomas, Ambroise, 65, 152
Toronto, Ontario, 135, 138, 170
Trincano, Mother, 27-29

Valletta, Malta, 57, 58
Van Horne, William, 122, 155
Venice, Italy, 92, 93, 112, 153
Verdi, Giuseppe, 150, 158, 159

International Star

Victoria, Queen, 3-17, 31, 61, 71, 72, 80, 90, 95, 96, 98, 104, 111, 119, 120, 126, 131-134, 137-139, 141, 147, 153, 157, 1518, 161, 162, 170, 171
Vittorio Emmanuele II, King (of Italy), 59, 93, 148-150, 153

Wagner, Richard, 90, 94, 97, 98, 112, 113, 123, 128, 132, 148, 154, 156

Wilhelm I, Emperor (of Germany), 100, 139, 150, 152, 158
Wilhelm II, Emperor (of Germany), 111, 158
Windsor Castle, 5, 10, 11, 17, 132, 133, 153
World War I, *See* First World War
Wüllner, Franz, 94

179

*Printed in November 2001
at AGMV/Marquis,
Cap-Saint-Ignace (Québec).*